SECOND WIND

GOLDEN FILLY SERIES

SECOND WIND

LAURAINE SNELLING

BETHANY HOUSE PUBLISHERS
MINNEAPOLIS, MINNESOTA 55438

Post-it is a registered trademark of the 3M Corporation.

Cover by Dan Thornberg,
Bethany House Publishers staff artist.

Published by Bethany House Publishers
A Ministry of Bethany Fellowship, Inc.
11300 Hampshire Avenue South
Minneapolis, Minnesota 55438

Printed in the United States of America

Library of Congress Cataloging-in-Publication Data

CIP applied for

ISBN 1–55661–401–2   CIP

To my mother.

Cheerleader, friend,

confidante,

and my shining example of

love in action.

LAURAINE SNELLING is a full-time writer who has authored a number of books, both fiction and non-fiction, as well as written articles for a wide range of magazines and weekly features for local newspapers. She also teaches writing courses and trains people in speaking skills. She and her husband, Wayne, have two grown children and make their home in California.

Her lifelong love of horses began at age five with a pony named Polly and continued with Silver, Kit, Rowdy, and her daughter's horse Cimeron, which starred in her first children's book *Tragedy on the Toutle*.

CHAPTER ONE

Why is it when everything finally starts going great again, something changes? Tricia Evanston chewed on the question as she settled into her favorite green canvas director's chair in Adam Finley's office at Bay Meadows Race Track. She heaved a sigh of relief. Morning works had gone smoothly—for a change. But something wasn't right. Like a hunter sniffing the air, she could sense it.

Her brother David entered, rubbing his shoulder. "That horse should be sent to the glue factory."

Trish tucked her chin to hide the smile she couldn't resist. Gatesby was up to his old tricks. David had forgotten to duck.

"He's just playing." She toyed with the end of her dark thick braid to keep from chuckling at the disgust on her brother's face.

"Yeah, well tell him to go play somewhere else, with someone else."

"Now, be honest. Think how much you'll miss him." She waved a hand to encompass the early morning track activity. "And all the rest of this when you're stuck in a library studying your brains out." Trish leaned back in her chair, one booted ankle crossed over the opposite knee. "Think of all the chemistry and yucky stuff you have to do."

"You forget. I like chemistry, not like someone else we all know and love." David tapped on the toe of her dusty boot.

"Here, you two. Have a bagel. We bought extra this morning in honor of David's last day." Owner/trainer Adam Finley opened the cardboard box and pulled the lids off the plastic containers of cream cheese. "I bought some of each so you children wouldn't have to fight for your favorites."

"Children! I like that." Trish bounded to her feet and tried to muscle David away from the box. "I want the raisin bagel with raisin-walnut cream cheese."

David grabbed her choice and held it up in the air. "What'll you give me?"

"A sock in the gut, you goof." Trish drew back her fist.

"Children, children, I thought we settled this long ago." Marge Evanston sailed through the door, shaking her head and grinning at the same time. "You'd think they'd act more grown-up by now, wouldn't you?" She winked at Adam, who watched the mock fight with a twinkle in his blue eyes.

"And you thought we invited you here for a serious meeting, right?" Adam smiled his welcome and rose to offer Marge his chair.

"Right. Trish, David gets to choose first. He probably won't be able to find bagels in Tucson, not that he'll have any time to look." Marge snagged a plain bagel out of the box and applied the vegetable cheese spread to the circular bread.

"He always gets to choose first, just 'cause he's bigger." Trish retrieved her bagel from her brother's grasp and handed him the one she knew he liked best. Licking cream cheese from her fingers, she pulled an orange juice from the refrigerator in the corner and leaped for her chair before David could steal it.

"You two sure are . . ."

"Full of the dickens?" Trish tried to look innocent.

"Better than what I was thinking." Marge slapped David's fingers away from her cup of coffee. "Thanks, Adam." She acknowledged the poured coffee. "Have they been like this every morning?"

"Naw. I think that finally winning a race has gone to Trish's head. And David? Well, you know what happens when you get on the wrong side of Gatesby."

Marge groaned. "The wrong side or any side. Did his teeth break the skin this time?"

David shook his head, his mouth too full of bagel to answer.

Trish swallowed. "What do you mean, gone to my head? I was fine 'til he showed up." She licked more cheese from her fingers and eyeballed her brother. The glow inside her had nothing to do with the spices in the cream cheese. Yes, she had won yesterday. She and Firefly. Finally. But today the good feeling came just because her family was together.

If only—she clamped a lid on the thought. *If only* usually triggered memories of her father, who'd died just as she and Spitfire won the Belmont, and thus the Triple Crown, in June. Now at the end of August she could sometimes think of him without crying. She rolled her eyes upward and sniffed quickly. She didn't want to make the others feel sad today. David would leave in the morning for Tucson, Arizona, for his second year of college.

"Okay, let's get down to business." Adam pushed papers aside to set his coffee mug on the scarred wooden desk.

Trish blinked one more time. She'd won—barely.

She cocked her ankle over her knee again and locked her hands behind her head. Wouldn't it be something if they let her take Spitfire out of retirement and train him for the Breeder's Cup? Oh, to race the big, black colt again at Churchill Downs! She could feel the wind on her face . . . hear the crowd. She brought her attention back to the present with a thump.

"What do you mean, something funny's going on at Portland Meadows? I thought the season was a go . . . starting in September like always."

Marge shook her head. "I didn't want to have to tell you this until we got home, but there have been rumors."

"What kind of rumors?" Trish leaned her elbows on her denim-clad knees.

"Like the track won't open for one thing." David wiped his mouth with a napkin. "But, you know, we've heard that before."

"So, what's new?" Trish stared from her mother to her brother and over to Adam.

"Some say it's just bad management, but . . ." Marge twisted her wedding ring on her finger.

"But. . . ?" Trish felt as if the starting gun was about to go off and her mount wasn't ready.

"But I don't know." Marge lifted a troubled gaze to her daughter. "I have a funny feeling, but I haven't had time to follow through on anything."

"What does Patrick think?" Since her father had hired the old jockey as trainer, Trish had grown to trust the Irishman's opinion.

Marge looked to David, as if seeking help.

"He thinks we should leave these horses down here until things are straightened out. Maybe ship some others down if we have to." David combed restless fingers through his dark, curly hair.

"But how could I ride then and still go to school?" Trish clamped her teeth against the rush of dread. They couldn't close The Meadows. They just couldn't. Not now when she'd finally won again and decided God wanted her to keep racing.

"That's why I haven't said anything. You know what your father always said about borrowing trouble. You could fly down here on the weekends, I guess." Marge shrugged. "There are no easy answers, Tee."

"But is the Thoroughbred Association doing anything about the situation?"

Marge shrugged again. "As I said, I haven't had time to follow any of this to the source."

Trish could tell her mother was feeling a bit pushed about the entire situation. What a bummer. Here she was, just beginning her senior year at Prairie High School. She couldn't miss a lot of classes this year. It was too important. Besides, she and her forever-friend Rhonda had so many plans.

"There's nothing you can do about it now," David said just before he stuffed the last of his bagel in his mouth. "We need to talk about the Breeder's Cup."

"Aye, that we do." Adam brushed a hand over his shiny dome, fringed by a fluff of white hair. "I plan on taking two horses to run that weekend, and I think Firefly has as good a chance as any in the Down's Handicap on Saturday. She ran well yesterday, and both Carlos and I think she's just coming into her own. I'd be glad to take her with us about ten days ahead, and Trish can fly in on that Thursday or Friday before."

"Who would you get to work them for you?" Trish hated the idea of someone else riding her horses in the morning. She should be the one doing that. She sneaked a peek at her mother.

"Don't even think it." Marge didn't crack a smile.

Trish shrugged. "As Dad always said, 'It doesn't hurt to dream.'" She turned to Adam. "Wouldn't it be something if we could run Spitfire in the Breeder's Cup? That was another of Dad's dreams, you know, having an entry in the Breeder's Cup."

"Sorry, Trish, you know our syndicate would never go along with that. Spitfire's too valuable at stud to risk an injury. Just think, maybe in three years you'll be running one of his sons at Churchill Downs."

Trish cupped her hands around her elbows. "Won't that be something?" She gave a wriggle of anticipation. "What if one of his colts, or even a filly, won the Triple Crown? I can just see it now."

David snapped his fingers in front of her eyes. "Calling Trish . . . come in Trish. We're talking about right now. You can dream about another Triple Crown on your own time."

"Oh." She flashed her brother a brilliant grin. "Okay, okay, back to the present. You already know I would love to take Firefly to Kentucky." She turned to Adam.

"How about asking Red to ride for you? I'm sure he'll be riding there then." Trish felt a tingle race around her middle and gallop out to her fingers. Red Holloran had to be the nicest—no, not a good enough word—the sexiest, that's what Rhonda called him, sweetest, most fun. . . . She clamped off the words. Face it, she *really* liked that certain redheaded jockey. Just think, if she could spend two weeks back there. . . . Her mind took off again.

"What about keeping the rest of our horses down here until we know what's happening up in Portland?" Marge asked. "Patrick suggested you might race the others too if Portland Meadows doesn't open."

Trish reentered reality with a thump. She carefully hid her thoughts behind a nod and a smile. If nobody else in their family was going to fix things at Portland Meadows, she'd look into it. There had to be a way to have racing in Portland this winter.

"That's decided then." Adam started writing on a pad on his desk. "I'll be sending my entries in today. You better do the same. I have extra forms here if you'd like." He dug in the file cabinet to his left and pulled out a file folder.

With the forms filled out, Marge rose to her feet. "Thanks, Adam, for all the care you've given us. You have no idea how much your friendship and advice, let alone keeping Trish down here, has meant." She extended her hand, but instead of shaking it, Adam pulled her into a hug.

"You've become like family to us, my dear. We couldn't have done any differently." His voice cracked on the words.

Trish felt that old familiar lump take up residence in her throat again. It threatened to choke her when she recognized the sheen of tears in her mother's eyes. She hugged her knees to her chest. Outside, down the line of green-painted stalls, a horse whinnied. Another answered.

"Thank you." Marge stepped back and drew a tissue

from the pocket of her tan slacks. After blowing her nose, she tucked the tissue back and picked up her purse. "Martha and I are going to church. Anyone care to join us?"

"I'll go." David made a bank shot into the trash with his napkin and stood up.

"Tee?"

"I need to be back by noon. I ride in the fifth and seventh today."

"Good. Then we'll be able to worship together for a change." Marge turned to Adam. "You coming?"

"I'm right ahead of you." He stepped outside and told Carlos, the head groom, he'd be leaving.

When they all walked back to the parking lot, Trish shoved her hands in the back pockets of her jeans. After today, it would be just she and her mother. She cut off the sad thoughts and nudged David with her hip. Teasing him always made her feel better.

"We need to call the Shipsons to ask if we can come," she said to her mother as they reached the cars.

"Later—after church."

———

Trish forced her mind to concentrate on the service. Her thoughts kept skipping ahead to the visit with Spitfire. Every time she left him, she was afraid he would forget her.

Marge handed Trish the hymnbook as they rose to their feet. The look she gave her daughter left no doubt that she knew where Trish's mind roamed.

The young pastor stepped into the pulpit and looked over the congregation. His gaze seemed to stop at Trish, as if speaking right to her. "Let not your heart be troubled. . . . In my Father's house are many mansions: if it were not so, I would have told you." He closed the Bible and leaned forward.

Trish gritted her teeth and kept her eyes on the speaker. That had been one of her father's favorite verses. He often spoke of his Father's mansions. But when she tried to picture him there, she always felt the tears.

"What a comfort," the pastor said, "to know we will see our loved ones again. They are there waiting for us. Cheering us on. You know that chorus the children sing? 'Heaven is a wonderful place.' What a promise Jesus gave us!"

Marge slipped her hand into Trish's. She took David's on the other side and squeezed. Shoulder to shoulder, the three of them faced forward, still a family in spite of their loss.

Trish looked up to see the sun streaming through the stained-glass window of the shepherd with a lamb. The beams of light glinted off the gold cross on the altar, as if to restate the promise. When the organ music rose in the final hymn, Trish felt as if she'd truly been in a holy place. Her heart swelled along with the song. "Thank you, Father," Trish whispered under the strains of music. "I needed this."

———

That afternoon at the track Trish continued to feel the peace she'd found in church. While the colt under her danced and pranced his way to the starting gate, she entertained him with her song. The horse flicked his ears and snorted but walked flat-footed into the gate.

Trish settled herself and him, a smile on her face and the song still singing in her heart.

The gate flew open. The gray colt broke. Trish exploded along with him and drove him toward the turn. With only six furlongs, they had no time to fool around.

The colt lengthened his stride. Neck and neck with a horse on their right, they left the field behind and headed for the finish line. Stride for stride the two dueled down the stretch. The other rider went to the whip. Trish leaned forward and sang into her mount's ears, "Go, fella, you can do it. Come on now, baby."

The colt lengthened his stride again. He pulled forward by a head, a neck, and then the contender disappeared behind them. Trish and her mount surged across the finish line two lengths in the lead. Trish let him slow down, her jubilation punctuated with a "thank you, God" at the top of her lungs.

Back at the Finleys' condo that evening Trish called the Shipsons in Kentucky. When they learned of Trish's plan, they responded with delight. Trish hung up the phone and turned to Marge. "They can't wait until we get there. Mrs. Shipson—Bernice—is thrilled you are coming along." Trish danced a step and shuffle in delight. They were going to see Spitfire. "I better send Red a letter to let him know."

"Too late." David lay back on the couch. He stretched his arms above his head. "He'll be too busy to see you anyway." He ducked when Trish thumped him with the pillow. "Mother, call off your kid," David laughed.

"Guess I'll call him then." Trish flipped through her address book for the Holloran number and headed for the bedroom to make the call in private. After her conversation, she returned to the living room. "He's racing at Keeneland, his mother said. She'll let him know I called."

"Did you ask how he's doing? Racewise, that is," Marge asked from her place in the corner of the eight-foot couch.

"Better than me, that's for sure. Guess he's been in the money most of the summer. Mrs. Holloran says they haven't seen much of him at all."

"Will he be riding at Louisville?" Adam asked.

"I guess." Trish refused to look at her brother when she heard his snort. She could feel the warmth begin at her collarbone and work its way upward. David could always make her blush about Red. "You leaving before works or after?" She felt like bopping him with the pillow again. A couple of times, just to let him know how much she cared.

"About the time you do. That's a long haul to Tucson." David stretched again and rose to his feet. "The car's all packed." He crossed the room to Margaret Finley's rocker. "Thank you for all you've done for me. After staying with you, I know why Trish calls this her second home."

Margaret set her needlepoint on the floor and stood to give him a hug. "You come back anytime. The farm is even closer to you than this, so if you need a weekend away from school, just let us know." She stood on tiptoe to kiss his cheek. "I'll bake an apple pie just for you."

"See you in the morning, son." Adam waved from his laid-back recliner. "Just remember, if you ever need a job, there's always an opening with me."

"We have first dibs on him." Marge uncurled her legs

and stood. "See you all in the morning. Come on, you two. I'll tuck you in."

The three followed one another up the stairs.

Trish told David good-night at the door and preceded her mother into the bedroom they shared. "You want to go shopping in the morning after works at the track? Tomorrow's my day off."

"Is this my Trish inviting her mother to go shopping?" Marge raised her eyebrows in mock surprise.

"Rhonda and I had a blast. We could too."

"I know. We will. And if we keep busy enough, maybe I'll be able not to think about David and his trek for a few minutes."

"Bad, huh?" Trish sank down on the edge of the bed. "Me too. I keep hoping things will go back to normal, but I can't find normal anymore."

CHAPTER TWO

Surely it was the fog making her eyes water.

David hugged his mother one last time and then Trish. "Take care of yourself, twerp." He tapped the end of her nose and grinned—a jaunty grin that didn't quite make it to his eyes. "Bye all." He waved and slid behind the wheel of his car, which matched Trish's red LeBaron convertible.

Trish heard Marge sniff as the red taillights disappeared in the fog. *Please take good care of him, God,* Trish prayed as she blew her nose. *And us. Our family just keeps getting smaller.*

Adam laid a hand on her shoulder and squeezed. He too seemed to be suffering from early foggy morning nose dripping. Trish revised her prayer. Maybe their family was really getting bigger.

"You could go back to bed for a few hours," she told her mother as she and Adam prepared to leave for the track. "One of us needs plenty of sleep before we attack those stores."

Marge wiped her eyes and shivered in the chill. "Think I will. Unless I could do something for you at the track."

Trish caught her jaw before it bounced on her chest.

Was this really *her* mother talking? "Thanks, but you sleep. See you around ten or so."

Trish checked the clock on the dashboard as she turned the ignition. Ten to five. They were running late. She followed Adam's taillights down the hill and past the guarded entry to the condominium complex. Once on El Camino Real, the golden light from the fog-piercing streetlamps shone on the early commuters.

Trish let her mind fly north to Portland and the problems at Portland Meadows. Somebody had to do something, but what? And who? Was there really something going on that shouldn't be?

She tucked those thoughts away when she parked her car in the parking lot and got out to walk with Adam to the stalls. If she allowed her mind to really wander, it would head back home for a few more snoozes.

The morning passed without a hitch. Gatesby even acted like a gentleman, rubbing his forehead against her chest rather than sneaking in a nip or three. Trish followed Adam's instructions and warmed up Sarah's Pride before letting her out at the half-mile pole to breeze her. She mentally ticked off the seconds as the poles blurred by and pulled the excited filly down again at the mile. They trotted back to the exit gate, the filly pulling at the bit all the while.

"You've come a long way, girl," Trish sang to the twitching ears as the filly kept track of everything going on around her. "You behave real well now. Wait 'til Patrick sees you." Sarah's Pride snorted and tossed her head, sending bits of foamy spit flying into Trish's face.

Trish wiped off a glob with a gloved hand and settled back into the saddle as Adam fell into step with them.

"Well, what do you think?" His blue eyes twinkled

when he looked up at the girl on the horse.

"Fourteen and seven tenths." Trish named the time she estimated they'd used.

Adam shook his head. "You amaze me. For one so young . . ." He held up the stopwatch. You were only five tenths of a second off. That's about your best time." He patted the filly on the shoulder. "And you did right well, young lady. Nice to see you mind your manners."

"You've a stakes race for her this time, right?" Trish kept a firm hand on the reins. She wanted no surprises this morning.

"Umm-humm." Adam nodded and smiled greetings to everyone who walked past. Whether he admitted it or not, he was a popular person, not to mention a respected trainer at Bay Meadows. "I thought she was ready, and this breeze proves me right. She's well conditioned, and I think we've broken her bad habits. We'll see if Patrick knows his stuff, won't we?"

Patrick O'Hern, the ex-jockey/trainer her father had hired and who was now helping Runnin' On Farm build a larger string, had recommended they put an offer on Sarah's Pride in a claiming race at Pimlico. He saw the potential, and her father had agreed.

"She's lookin' good," Carlos, the head groom, said when Trish jumped to the ground. "Your agent came by . . . said for you to call him."

"Gracias, Carlos." Trish ducked under the filly's neck and headed for the office. She only had Gimmeyour-heart to work and she'd be finished. Hopefully, her agent had plenty of mounts for her this week.

She felt like spinning round and round, like a top flashing reds and golds in its humming dance. Friday evening they'd be flying to Kentucky to see Spitfire.

Her imaginary top wobbled and toppled over. After Friday she wouldn't be racing for—for who knew how long. Here she'd been nearly ready to quit, and now the thought of it made her throat tighten. Would she ever understand herself?

She finished marking the four mounts her agent had for her in her calendar and stuffed it back into her pack. That gave her nine mounts in four days. Things were looking up.

After riding Gimmeyourheart, Trish forced him to walk back to the stables. "He acts like he has no idea what he's supposed to do out there," she said as she kicked her right foot out of the irons and slid to the ground. "No wonder he didn't do well."

"Maybe he was just testing you." Carlos stripped off the saddle and cloth while Juan, Trish's favorite stable-boy, prepared a soapy, warm water bucket. "What about that hoof?"

"Feels like he favors it. You sure it's all healed?"

"Maybe we should send him out to the farm and let him loose for a while. Since you don't know whether Portland will start or not in a couple of months, let's give him another rest." Adam checked each hoof and felt for any heat in the fetlocks. "Seems fine but . . ." He shook his head. "You watch . . . when he comes back, he'll be a sizzler."

Trish hoped the doubt didn't show on her face.

When she got back in her car, the first thing she saw was PTL! written in huge letters on a Post-it she'd stuck to her dash earlier. Praise the Lord. She'd promised to do just that—in everything—as the Bible said and her father had done. Nagger seemed to stretch and uncurl on her shoulder to chuckle in her ear. *What's it been? Two days? Three? And no praise. I told you you couldn't do it. Or wouldn't.*

Trish wished she could brush him away like a pesky fly. She studied the slip of pink paper. Good reminder. She turned the ignition and put the car into gear. "I will praise the Lord. Thank you for the sunshine." That one was easy. "Thank you for taking care of David as he travels." That one was hard. "I praise you for helping me win again." Super easy.

Streets and stores, cars and pedestrians, flashed past in her peripheral vision as she struggled to find ten things to be grateful for. She had only promised to do three a day, but she had several days to make up for. "Thank you, Jesus, that Mom is here and we are going shopping." Easy. She pushed her black sunglasses up on her nose with one finger. Portland. How could she praise God for the mess in Portland? She tried the words out several ways. Nothing felt right. She sucked in a deep breath as if she were preparing to dive. "Thank you that you know what is happening up there and you can . . ." She paused. Yes, God *could* take care of things. But would He?

She saluted the guard at the gate to the condominiums and drove on up the hill. Marge waved at her from the front door. Trish grabbed her bag and leaped up the steps. *Thank you for my mother.* That was certainly a lot easier now than it used to be.

———

Marge was as totally overwhelmed by the Stanford Mall as Trish and Rhonda had been.

"You ever think that you can afford to buy from any of these stores now?" Trish asked as they looked from

Neiman Marcus to I. Magnin and over to Saks.

Marge turned, shaking her head as she answered. "But why would I want to? I don't really *need* anything."

"I know. But you could if you wanted to." Trish took her mother by the arm. "I guess it's just that all these years you've made do, bought stuff for us kids when we needed it and not something you needed because we couldn't afford both. Now I want to buy *you* something for a change. I can afford it."

"So can I."

"Too bad. It's not the same. You want to hit the fancy stores or see where Rhonda and I found our cool outfits?"

Marge squeezed Trish's hand against her side. "Both."

By three o'clock the number of packages had grown to fill all four of their arms. "You know that phrase 'Shop 'til you drop?' " Marge set her shopping bags down on the sidewalk.

Trish nodded as she followed her mother's actions.

"I dropped . . . about an hour ago." Marge shrugged her shoulders and rubbed her hand where the bags' skinny handles had dug a groove. "And I'm starved."

"Me too. Let's take this stuff to the car, and then I know of a super-good deli. Their dessert tray is to die for."

"Sounds good to me." They wended their way across the palm-tree-studded parking lot to the red convertible. Marge helped Trish put the packages in the trunk and then sank down on the car seat. "How come shopping makes me more tired than cleaning house all day, even doing the windows?"

"Yeah, I'd rather muck stalls for four hours." Trish

leaned against the front fender. She clasped her hands above her head and twisted from side to side. "That rust suit and hat will be a standout in the winner's circle at Churchill Downs. You're movie star material in it." Trish turned to look—really look—at her mother. "You know, Mom, if you wanted to, you could—"

Marge held up a hand. "Don't say it. I am not going to color my hair or fuss with my makeup or wear the latest style. That's just not me."

"That rust suit is pretty stylish." Trish rolled her lips to keep from laughing. "Come on, Mom, ya gotta go with the flow."

Marge heaved herself to her feet. "Just flow me to food before I flow right down the drain from hunger." She stopped when they started back across the asphalt. "You think maybe I better take that suit along so we can find some shoes to match?"

Trish locked her arm in her mother's. "It's right here in the bag." She swung the shopping bag she carried in her other hand. "And you need boots too."

"We're going to have to buy another suitcase for me to take all this home," Marge pretended to grumble.

"That's okay. I know where the luggage store is. I had to find one for Rhonda, remember?"

———

Later that night, after showing all their treasures to Margaret, Trish and her mother sat out on the deck watching the moon come up over the Eastbay hills. The evening breeze rustled in the palm fronds as birds twerped and tweeted in the branches, settling in for the night.

Trish lifted her face to catch the scent of jasmine

drifting from the ground cover on the hill beyond them.

"You have time to take me to the airport on Wednesday?" Marge lay back on the green and white padded chaise lounge. "Oh, this smells so good."

"Wednesday. Why don't you just fly out of here with me on Friday? There's no sense making two flights if you don't have to."

"But I have so much to do at home."

"It'll wait. Besides, Patrick can handle everything with the horses. Consider this your vacation." Trish closed her eyes and breathed in deeply. When a yawn caught her unaware, she patted her mouth and yawned again.

"Sounds like you're about ready for bed."

"I know. So what do you think?"

"I'm too comfortable to think. I'll play Scarlet O'Hara and think about it tomorrow." Marge stretched full length, like a kitten awaking from a deep sleep. "I'll stay. Now that I even have clothes to wear, who needs to go home?"

"Great!" Trish swung her feet to the deck. "If you want my car in the morning to go shopping . . ."

Marge groaned.

" . . . or anything, I can ride with Adam." Trish stood up. "And if you stay out here much longer, the mosquitoes will get you." She slapped at one on her arm. "Goodnight."

Finding three things to be thankful for was easy when Trish said her prayers: shopping, the peaceful look on her mother's face, and the call from David saying he'd made it safely. "Thank you that I get to see Spitfire on Friday." She paused. "And you are taking care of the mess in Portland, aren't you? Amen." She heard her mother return from the bathroom. "Night, Mom."

"Night, Trish." Marge stopped at her daughter's bed and bent down for a good-night kiss. "God loves you and so do I."

Trish felt the immediate rush of tears to the back of her eyes. Her father had always said that to her along with a good-night hug. "Me too." She swallowed the quiver in her voice and turned on her side. Margaret Finley had said the tears came unbidden for years after losing someone you love. And for Trish it had only been months. But at least they stopped now and the pain was more like an ache.

———

The week flew by with Trish winning one race, placing in two, coming up with a show, and at least getting paid for running the others around the track. The day she won she found tons to be grateful for . . . and the others? Well, as the psalmist David said, praise sometimes was a sacrifice.

Thursday night Trish closed her Bible after reading a couple of psalms where David moaned and groaned. But he always praised God somewhere in them. She hadn't been in the top four in either race. Moaning looked good.

But her heart felt overflowing with praises. Tomorrow she would see Spitfire.

In the morning Gatesby nearly left her a painful reminder to pay attention, but his teeth closed only on her shirt. "Whew. That was close." Trish jerked on his halter and shook her finger at him. "You want to be sent home, you dopey horse? I thought you were my friend."

"He's laughing at you," Juan said, his Mexican accent

more pronounced around his giggle.

"I know. And you are too because this time you weren't the target." Trish tried to glare at him, but her mouth wouldn't stay straight. The corners kept tipping up in a grin.

"Sí." Juan rubbed his shoulder. "From yesterday."

Trish kept her eyes and ears open wide for the rest of the morning. She sure didn't need any accidents to mess up this day. Their flight left at one. She said goodbye to all the horses, with a special reminder to Firefly to keep improving. Her big chance was coming up in October.

"I'll see you all next Friday night." She paused in the door to the office. "You want anything from Kentucky?"

"Get outta here." Adam shooed her out the door. "And you be nice to that certain redheaded jockey. He might not know how to handle a California girl."

Trish felt the blush start flaming on her neck and explode to her cheekbones. She shook her head as she jogged out to the parking lot. Would she be a blusher for the rest of her natural life? The wind in her face felt especially good while she drove back to the condo.

———

Trish stared out the window of the 727, the words "California girl" stuck on continuous replay in her mind. She leaned her head back against the seat, listening to the roar of the plane's engines, and tried to relax. Had she changed this summer? Would Red still like her as much as he said in the cards he wrote? Would she still like him?

CHAPTER THREE

Dark had overrun dusk by the time they landed in Lexington.

Donald and Bernice Shipson met them with hugs and laughter when they came off the plane.

"He's fine," Donald Shipson answered Trish's question before she could ask it. "I'd have brought him along if there were any way possible." He took Marge's carry-on bag and led them off to the baggage claim.

The drive to BlueMist Farms seemed like a transcontinental trip. Trish could feel her foot pressing against the floorboard as if she could make the car go faster by sheer willpower. They drove directly to the parking area near the stallion barn. A mercury light cast a blue-white sheen on the crushed gravel, but it was no rival for the moon riding high in the sky. The cupolaed stallion barn threw its own hulking shadow. A carriage lamp glowed golden against the white barn wall.

"Do you think he'll remember me?" Trish voiced the doubt that had crept in when she wasn't looking.

"The horse that tips all but Runnin' On Farm hats? You watch. He'll be as excited as you are." The tall, elegantly slim horse owner shook his head. "That is one smart stud we have there. He figured out how to open

29

his stall one day. Followed Timmy right out the door. So now we put a horse-proof fastener on it."

Trish felt like skipping and twirling down the wide path. Not too long now till she saw Spitfire. As they neared the barn Trish whistled, the high-low tone with which she always called her horses. She waited for only a breath before she heard a stallion's penetrating whistle followed by Spitfire's whinny. She would recognize it anywhere. He called again. She could hear him banging a hoof against the stall wall.

"I think your friend is calling you." Donald Shipson beckoned toward the barn door. "Come on, I'll turn on the lights."

Trish whistled again as she reached the door, this time softly. Spitfire's nicker brought tears to her eyes. It felt like years since she'd seen him, even though it had been less than two months.

Spitfire blinked in the sudden light, but he tossed his head and nickered again as if Trish couldn't get there quickly enough. His nostrils quivered in a soundless love call. Trish buried her face in his thick, coarse mane and hung on, letting her tears wet the shiny black coat.

Spitfire heaved a sigh as if he too had come home. He rested his head on her shoulder and closed his eyes when her fingers found all his favorite scratching places. Trish stroked his ears and down his cheek. After her tears dried, she turned around so she could really look at him. "How ya doin', big guy?" Spitfire raised his nose so she would scratch under his chin. Trish tickled his whiskers and giggled when he whiskered her hand.

"I don't even have a carrot for you." She stroked her hands down his face and rubbed up around his ears.

Spitfire leaned against her and closed his eyes again.

"Not keeping you up too late, am I?" Trish used her fingertips to tickle his whiskery upper lip. Spitfire licked her hand and whuffled at the familiar scent. When Trish raised her head, she caught the gleam of tears in her mother's eyes.

"Guess he remembers me, huh?" Trish swallowed the last of her own tears and hugged her horse again. "Tomorrow we'll go for a ride, okay?" But when she stepped away, he nickered and pawed the straw in his huge box stall.

"You may have to spend the night down here," Bernice Shipson said with a smile. "And here I have your room all ready for you."

Trish stepped back and let Spitfire rub his forehead on her chest. "Now you go back to sleep and I'll see you in the morning." She shoved his head away. "Go on now, you heard me." Spitfire tossed his head, his forelock swinging in the motion. But this time when she moved away, he just stood there, dark eyes alert, nostrils quivering.

"It's okay. I'll be here to feed you in the morning." Trish backed away. Spitfire pawed once, then stood perfectly still, the tips of his ears nearly touching as he watched Trish leave. He whinnied again after they closed the door, and then silence.

"Seems he knows every word you say." Donald Shipson shook his head. "You two are some pair."

"My dad always said Spitfire and I were soul mates from when he was foaled. We just understand each other." Trish took her place in the backseat of the car. *Thank you, God.* Her prayer wafted silently upward. She'd mentioned her father without tearing up. That had to be a first.

Trish fell asleep counting her blessings. Today had been easy to find three things—last count she remembered was eleven. But then, who was counting?

———

Early morning in Kentucky fell soft on her skin as Trish jogged down to the stallion barn. A bright red cardinal serenaded her from a stately elm tree, then flitted across the sloping drive and sang the chorus to his mate. The rising sun cast glittering diamonds on the grass bent with dew. Off in a manicured paddock, two babies kicked up their heels and raced the fence line. Trish inhaled a breath of pure joy. While later in the day it would be hot and muggy, right now felt soft like thistledown.

She heard a stallion trumpet, but it wasn't Spitfire's voice.

Someone whistled a happy tune from the barn ahead of her. Trish stopped and threw her three-tone whistle into the air, a gift to the horse she came to visit.

Spitfire answered immediately. A full-blown whinny, not just a nicker. He whinnied again and Trish heard a hoof bang the wooden wall.

"Easy now, me boyo, easy." A man's voice, with the words sounding more like "aisey," told Trish that Timmy O'Ryan, Spitfire's personal groom, was already in attendance.

Trish strode through the open door, bits of carrots she'd begged from the kitchen stuffed in her pockets. Spitfire, his entire being concentrated on the door, tossed his head and nickered again. With his head out the stall, he pushed against the blue webbing gate as if to lunge out to her.

"Morning, Trish. Donald said you'd be down early."

Timmy left off brushing the glossy black coat and joined Spitfire at the gate.

"Hi, Timmy. Morning, Spitfire." Trish smoothed the black forelock and rubbed the colt's cheek.

"Himself here's been awaitin' for you. I went ahead and fed him since I knew you'd want to ride."

"Thanks. How ya doin', fella?" Trish held out two carrot pieces. Spitfire snuffled her hair and blew in her face before lipping the carrots. As he crunched, he rested his forehead against her chest so she could reach his ears easily.

"You big baby." Trish rubbed all his favorite places while she talked. "Been a while since anyone's been on your back. You gonna behave yourself?" Spitfire nuzzled her pocket for another carrot.

"I'll get him saddled and then bring around a mount." Timmy pushed his porkpie hat back on his head. "He sure is happy to see you."

"I'll saddle him, if you don't mind."

"Not at all." The slim man, garbed all in tan but for shiny black boots, crossed to the tack room and returned with an English saddle, pad, and bridle. "You don't need a racing saddle on him now, or would you rather have one?"

"No, that's fine." Trish took the saddle from him and set it over the half door of the stall. "Come on, fella, let's get ready to see the country."

While Trish set the saddle in place and hooked the girth, Spitfire watched her over his shoulder, as if not wanting her out of his sight. When she led him outside, he sighed and nuzzled her shoulder.

"You be careful now . . . no nipping." Trish let him droop his head over her shoulder while they waited for

Timmy to join them. She stroked his nose, all the while murmuring the singsong she'd trained him with. Love words with their own special meaning. The colt's eyes drooped and his chin sank lower.

"Hard to believe he's that same ball of fire that won the Triple Crown." The groom led his mount up and stopped to give Trish a boost into the saddle. Then he swung aboard his horse and led the way down a lane between two black board fences that stretched over the gently rolling hills.

When they returned, Donald Shipson met them in the exercise ring off to the side of the two-story barn. "Breakfast's ready, Trish, so how about letting Timmy cool him out and brush him down? We're running today at Keeneland and thought maybe you and your mother would like to join us. Bernice says not to tell you our surprise."

Trish swung to the ground and let Spitfire rub his forehead against her shoulder. She had planned on spending more time with her horse, grooming and bathing him. She glanced up in time to see a wink flash between the two men. Something was up, all right.

She gave Spitfire the last carrot from her pocket and scratched between his ears while he munched. "See you later, fella. You be good now." Trish smoothed his forelock and handed Timmy the reins. "See you later, too."

Spitfire nickered as she climbed in the pickup with Mr. Shipson. When Trish waved, he raised his head and sent his shrill whinny floating after her.

"What surprise?" Trish turned to the man driving.

"I promised not to tell." Shipson looked as innocent as a kid with his hand in the cookie jar.

"Not fair."

"I know, but it sure is fun." His soft Kentucky drawl floated on the air.

"What races are you in?"

"Second and seventh. There's a three-year-old filly I think you should look at while we're there. Almost claimed her myself, but right now I don't need any new animals. Patrick asked me to keep my eyes open." Shipson parked the pickup in front of the pillared plantation house. "Sure hope you're hungry. Sarah outdid herself she was so glad to hear you were coming. Said she'd get you convinced southern cooking has no equal, one way or another."

Trish groaned. "If I ate all she wanted me to, I'd weigh enough for two jockeys." Together they climbed the three broad stairs to the double doors with a stained-glass fanlight above them.

Trish discovered the surprise when she joined the Shipsons in the saddling paddock for the second race. As the jockeys paraded down from the jockey room, Red Holloran stopped at stall number three.

Trish felt her stomach catch on her kneecaps going down and plunk about on her ankles. Yep, she still liked him. Her stomach didn't travel so far for *any* guy—just this one.

The grin that split his freckled face and the powerful arms that wrapped her in a hug told her the answer to her other question. Yep, he still liked her. When he let her loose, her face matched his hair. She could feel the heat, like a sunburn.

"You didn't know, did you?" Red asked as he kept her hand clasped in his.

"No, I wondered why there was no message at the Shipsons'. Then I was afraid you hadn't heard I was coming." Trish wished sheer mind control could cut the flaming in her cheeks. That and the current that sizzled up her arm.

"Riders up." The call echoed from the loudspeakers in the center of the paddock.

Red let go of her hand. "You'll still be here when I'm done?"

Trish nodded. "How many mounts do you have today?"

"Four, two for BlueMist." Red accepted the mount from Donald Shipson. "Pray me a win." He touched his whip to his helmet and away they went, Shipson leading until they picked up their pony rider.

When all eight entries filed out the tunnel, the group made their way to the owner's box. "He's not only an excellent jockey but a fine young man." Donald Shipson mounted the stairs beside Trish.

"Does he ride much for you?"

"Whenever I can get him. He's gotten pretty popular in the last few months. Good hand with the horses and developing real skill in bringing a horse out of the pack. I think he'll become one of the greats if he goes on like he has."

Trish thought about her last two months of not winning. Her father had said much the same about her and look what happened.

She watched across the infield to where the horses were entering the gates. As the shot fired, she sent her prayer for Red's safety heavenward.

It seemed so strange to be in the grandstand instead of down along the fence or, even better, mounted on one of the straining horses rounding the turn and making their first drive past the stands.

"He's right where I wanted him," Shipson said, his eyes fixed on the surging field. "Let that number one wear himself out with too fast a pace." He raised his binoculars as they moved into the backstretch.

Trish wished she'd brought some. It was easy to lose a bright red gelding in the midst of three others. And at that distance, the blue and white silks of BlueMist disappeared also.

Coming out of the turn, the blue and white silks on a bright red gelding pulled away from the two on either side and with each stride increased his lead. Red won by six lengths.

Trish heard herself screaming encouragement as the winner crossed the line and raised his whip in victory. She hugged her mother and danced in place until they paraded down to the winner's circle. This time, instead of standing in front of the horse, she joined the others on the risers behind. The camera flashed, the horse was led away, and she thumped Red on the arm as he accepted congratulations from the Shipsons.

"Thanks for the prayers," he whispered in her ear, all the while smiling and graciously acknowledging the good wishes from others around him.

"I only prayed for your safety, not a win." Trish smiled along with him.

"Thanks anyway. I'll see you after the seventh. Pray for more wins." He squeezed her hand and left to return to the jockey room.

He won again on Shipson's horse in the seventh, the largest race of the day. This time the excitement in the winner's circle crackled like an electric wire. Red had come from behind after a bad bump and won by only a nose.

Trish's heart still hammered after the near miss. She could tell that her *thank you, God* had been heartily joined with those of the Shipsons and her mother. Now she knew what it felt like to be helpless in the stands when someone you cared about fought their way around the track.

"Thanks again." Red pulled a red rose from the bouquet he held and handed it to her. "You prayed the best way."

Trish held the bloodred blossom to her nose. The sweet fragrance overlaid the smell of horse and sweat and fear. "You're welcome." She pushed the words past the lump in her throat.

"You'll join us for dinner, won't you, son?" Donald Shipson asked.

"Be glad to, sir," Red answered. "Is it all right if Trish rides with me?" At Marge's nod, he turned back to Trish. "I'll meet you right here then?"

"How about down at barn fourteen? I want them to see that filly of Orson's. She was scratched from the fifth today, but at least they can look at her."

"Fine. See you. Oh, and I rode that filly once. She's got heart but not enough condition." He waved again and trotted off to the jockey room.

———

Talk at the supper table revolved around the races of the day and then to the gray filly.

"I don't know," Marge answered. "If Portland Meadows doesn't open this fall, I guess we're shipping ours down to Adam Finley. I hate to take on another new horse when we're in such a state of confusion."

"What have you heard about the situation there?"

Shipson wiped his mouth with a snowy napkin. "Any change?"

Marge shook her head. "No one seems to know anything for sure."

"Rumor has it that The Meadows is already closed." Red leaned forward. "I hate to see another track go down."

"What about me? I'll have to commute to California to ride." Trish carefully refrained from looking at her mother. How would they ever run their horses only on the weekends when she could fly down there? "It just isn't fair."

Since when is life fair? Nagger whispered in her ear as if he'd been waiting for a chance to dig in his claws.

CHAPTER FOUR

The rest of the weekend passed in a blur. Before Trish knew it she was back on the plane, heading for Vancouver. School would begin in the morning.

She leaned back against the headrest and let her mind play with the scenes of the weekend. Red Holloran nearly nosed Spitfire out for first place. She'd see both of them again in October, less than a month away. And this Friday she would fly down to San Francisco to race on Saturday and drive back to Vancouver on Sunday.

"You're awfully quiet." Marge put down her magazine and turned to look at her daughter.

"Just thinking. I'm going to be really busy, aren't I?"

Marge smiled and nodded. "Seems that way to me."

Trish rubbed the bridge of her nose, unconsciously mimicking David's action when he was thinking. "You thought anymore about Portland Meadows?"

"Sort of. I figured we'd get this weekend out of the way first and then tackle the next item on the agenda." Marge accepted a glass of soda from the flight attendant and passed Trish her standard Diet Coke. "It's like I keep hoping the situation will resolve itself if I look the other way." She shook her head. "But that is rarely the case."

"We had a super weekend though." Trish sipped her

drink. "I'm really glad you came along."

"Thanks." Marge patted Trish's cocked knee. "Back to Portland Meadows. I'd just as soon you didn't get involved in the situation there, whatever the situation is."

"Are you telling me I can't talk to the other owners?" Trish felt a niggle of resentment settle around her chest.

"No, I'm giving you my opinion. I'd like you to have a sane and normal senior year with time to take part in all the activities."

"Thanks, Mom." Trish sipped her drink again. That had been close. She knew she'd want to make sure something was done about racing at PM. At least they weren't going to start out fighting about something so important as that. The thought of other jockeys riding their horses bothered her more than she wanted to admit. That was her job. But she sure couldn't do it if all the horses were based in California.

Dad, what would you do in this situation? Trish closed her eyes and leaned her seat back. If she sat real quiet, she could almost feel him sitting right beside her. He'd be reading the latest *Blood Horse Journal* or one of his "good books," as he called authors like Norman Vincent Peale.

He always said you could find your answers in the Scriptures if you looked hard enough. Trish rubbed her tongue on the back of her teeth. Where would she find a reference for horse racing?

Immediately a verse leaped into her mind. "Do unto others as you would have them do unto you." The golden rule. She wrinkled her eyebrows. What did that have to do with racing?

Their meal arrived and Trish poured dressing on her salad in an unconscious gesture. "Do unto others." It seemed as if they were being done unto and not in a good way. She ate her meal, all the while mulling over the verse. Another came into her mind. This one she could picture on her wall of 3×5 cards, all verses printed either by her or her father. "I can do all things through Christ who strengthens me." Now that one made more sense.

After giving her empty tray to the flight attendant, Trish flipped back the armrest and curled up in the double seat for a nap. She was just about out when she felt her mother spread one of the airline blankets over her. "Thanks, Mom," Trish mumbled.

When Trish and her mother walked off the plane, Patrick waited there to meet them. Trish nearly walked on by because the retired jockey stood behind a man tall enough to play professional basketball.

"You're going to have to stand in front of guys like that," Trish teased after they swapped hugs and started down the long walk to the baggage claim. "Or you'll get lost."

Patrick gave her a poke with his elbow. "And let's be lookin' at who's talking. He'd be taller'n you and Spitfire put together. Speaking of which, how's our son doin'?"

"Great." Trish turned with a grin. "And yes, you were right."

"And what might that be about?"

"He didn't forget me."

"I told you, that horse has a memory like an elephant. And he'll never be forgettin' ye. Yer the most important person in his life."

"I still wish we could race him again." Trish sighed.

"Give it up, lass. We'll bring on a young'un to do it again." Patrick stood back to let Trish and Marge step onto the escalator in front of him.

"What's happening at The Meadows?" Marge asked in an undertone because Trish stood three steps down in front of her.

"The Thoroughbred Association has called a meeting for Tuesday night. The city council is supposed to make a decision at their meeting on Thursday." Patrick tried to speak softly enough for Trish to miss it.

"But that's tomorrow night." Trish stepped to the side at the bottom of the escalator.

"I know." Marge and Patrick exchanged a look that told Trish they'd rather not discuss this now.

Fine, Trish thought. *I can play that game too. But tomorrow night Runnin' On Farm will be well represented at the meeting.* "They've started our luggage carousel" was all she said as she walked through the turnstile to stand by the moving luggage line.

On the way home, the three caught up on all the news of Runnin' On Farm. The new mare and filly they'd purchased from the breeder in Chehalis were settling in well. Miss Tee and Double Diamond had grown an inch a night, or so it seemed.

"We'll be working with the yearling Calloway's Joker soon as you get out to the barn. I'm too heavy for him and a'course Brad makes me look like a midget."

"Brad's already started school?" Trish leaned between the two front seats of the minivan.

"Nope. Later than you. But he's sure been a help these last couple of weeks. That boy's awful good with horses."

"He should be. Brad Williams nearly grew up at our place. He and David . . ." Marge shook her head. "And Trish and Rhonda. What those four couldn't think of."

"Come on, Mom, we weren't *that* bad."

"You won't believe the mountains of cookies I used to bake. Hal teased me about becoming a professional baker."

"You still could. Like Brad said, you make the best cinnamon rolls around." Trish leaned her elbows on her knees and her chin on the palms of her hands. "You think David likes the cooking at the dorm?"

"I doubt it. All college students complain about the food. There's a rule somewhere that says they have to." Marge turned in her seat. "We'll call him when we get home and let him know we got through the weekend all right."

Dusk colored the farm amethyst and faded the edges as they turned into the long, graveled driveway. The farm and family collie, Caesar, leaped and yipped beside the slow-moving van, doing his best to welcome them home.

The cedar-sided house lay to the right. Flower skirts of red and gold and pink flaunted their bursts of blooms before fall dimmed their glory. One last ray of golden sun reflected off the picture window, brassy and brilliant in the dusk.

Off to the left and down a bit lay the barns with the horse paddocks out behind. Patrick's mobile home, surrounded by another flower display, nestled against the rise as if it had lived there forever.

Trish felt a lump in her throat. Was coming home always the best part of a trip? It felt like she'd been gone for months, years maybe, instead of weeks.

Her father would be down at the paddocks, checking on the horses for the final time of the day. She sighed and blinked against the moisture that stung her eyelids.

If only that were true. How much she had to tell him. She rolled her lips together and pulled open the sliding door. But now, she had to keep on keeping on. He wasn't here and he wouldn't be.

Caesar planted both his front feet on her knee before she could slide out. The fastest tongue in the West caught her chin and the tip of her nose before she dug her fingers into his blazing white ruff and let him lick away the tears too. "You silly old dog." Trish shook her hands and Caesar grinned his doggie grin. "You missed me, huh?" Caesar dropped to all fours, yipped and ran around in a circle, scrabbling dirt into the air.

"I think he's glad to see you." Marge retrieved her purse from the van and chuckled at the dog's antics. "If you hurry, you can check on the horses before absolute dark."

Trish waved at her mom and trotted down the rise, her three-tone whistle calling both the dog and the horses. A whinny answered her and then another. Caesar ran in front of her, turned to bark, then dashed off again.

Trish dropped to a walk when she rounded the long, low stable and started down the lane between the board-fenced paddocks. Another whinny floated up to her on the evening breeze. Old, gray Dan'l, their now-retired-from-racing thoroughbred and her riding teacher, was welcoming her home. The second whinny had the young sound of Miss Tee or Double Diamond. Who had whistled like she did so they recognized it?

Ahead in the dimness, she could faintly see a gray horse standing with his head over the fence. He whinnied again. Trish ran down the lane, stopping just in time to walk up to the aging animal. "Hello, old man.

How ya doin'?" Dan'l whuffled, his nostrils fluttering in a soundless nicker. He sniffed her hand, her arm, and up to her cheek, then nosed at her pocket where she usually kept the carrots.

"None today, fella. I haven't even been in the house yet." She rubbed his ears and down his cheek. "You're lookin' good for such an old son." Dan'l nodded and blew in her face. He licked her cheek and hung his head low so she could rub the crest of his mane and between his ears. When he sighed, it was as if she'd never been away. Trish patted him again, then worked her way down the row of horse heads bobbing at the fence line.

Miss Tee and Double Diamond stood back aways and reached out to sniff her proffered hand. The new filly hung back even further. "Scaredy cats," Trish murmured, all the while keeping her hand palm down so they could sniff comfortably. "You'll have to learn to trust me again, you know. Mom's spoiled you, I bet."

Caesar shoved his nose into her hand and whined. The peeper frogs sang their nightly three-part chorus down by the swamp. Up above, three stars ran interference for the heavenly host to come as the sky deepened from cobalt to black.

Trish gave Dan'l an extra hug and strode back up the lane. Time to call Rhonda and plan their big entrance in the morning. And time to read the clippings Patrick had been saving about the mess at Portland Meadows.

"Patrick carried your luggage to your room," Marge said when Trish opened the sliding glass door from the deck behind the house. "We're going to have coffee in about five minutes if you want to join us."

"Okay. How about if I call Rhonda first?"

"You think you can talk for only five minutes?"

48

"Prob'ly not. But I can always call her back." Trish glanced into the living room at her father's recliner. So often he'd sat there reading his Bible or resting after he got so sick. A circle of light from the lamp beside it fell on the worn cushions. Even his patchwork quilt lay folded across the back. His worn black Bible occupied its usual place on the end table.

Trish walked quickly down the hall. She *would not* cry.

Her room wore the look of perfection only possible when she lived elsewhere. No jeans, sweatshirts, boots, or even tissues out of place. Everything dusted, the crimson and gold throw pillow not thrown but centered against the other pillows. She raised her gaze to the blank wall above her desk. The first thing she'd do when she got back from California on Sunday would be to pin all the cards with Bible verses back in place. Her mother had saved them from the trash.

Trish ignored the yawn that attacked her from the sight of the pillows and marched back down the hall to the kitchen. She might still be on Kentucky time, but now she had to function on Washington time, and here it was only eight o'clock. Time to call Rhonda. And later, Brad.

"Hi, Rhonda, it's me." Trish sank to the floor and propped her back against the corner of the door and the kitchen cabinets. "So, how's everything for the morning?" After telling Rhonda as much as possible about the Kentucky trip, Trish waved a hand at her mother. "I gotta go. Mom's dishing up peach pie and ice cream. You and Brad should be here. So I'll pick you up about twenty to eight, okay?" Trish hung up the phone and pushed herself to her feet. "Rhonda said to tell you hi and she's glad we're home."

"Here, you take the tray. We're going to eat in the living room for a change." Marge picked up the coffee carafe and followed Trish into the living room.

Patrick sat in the corner of the sofa, reading *Blood Horse* in the lamplight. He put the magazine down and smiled up at Trish. "Sure and it's good to have ye home, lass." He took the plate of dessert and set it down on the end table. "It's been lonely here, even though Brad came to help me. I got real spoiled having a family around all the time."

Marge handed him a coffee mug. "You need to be spoiled after all those years alone. Besides, you're making it easier for Trish and me too. This house seems mighty big for two women."

"Maybe we could bring Caesar in?" Trish grinned around the spoon she licked.

"And maybe not." Marge shook her head. "Some people will try anything. Finish your dessert, child. It's time for you to be in bed since you have school tomorrow."

Trish licked her ice cream from the spoon again. "You haven't gotten to say something like that for a long time." She turned to Patrick. "Used to be her famous last words every night." Trish caught herself in a big yawn. "And tonight you're right. Patrick, Mom said you'd been keeping the articles on The Meadows."

"Aye. But they're down at my house. I'll bring them up tomorrow. You sleep in. We'll work horses and I'll catch you up on the training we're doing after school."

"Good." Trish stretched and yawned again. "Night." She swallowed another yawn and, after kissing her mother good-night, ambled down the hall to her room.

While her bags needed unpacking, her mother had been kind enough to hang up the garment bag containing the new outfit for school in the morning. Trish unzipped the bag and drew out the hangers holding her new skirt, vest, and rust-colored silk blouse. The silver-toed western boots that finished off the outfit nestled in their wrapping in the stuffed bag on the floor. She hung the outfit on the door to let it shake out and undressed for bed.

After she crawled under the covers she heard Patrick leave and her mother's steps coming down the hall. Marge tapped on the half-open door and leaned her head in.

"You sleeping yet?"

"Nope." Trish patted the side of the bed. "Here."

Marge sat as invited and drew one knee up on the bed. She studied her daughter, a half smile playing across her face. "You have no idea how wonderful it is to see you here in your own bed again."

Trish wriggled and smiled back. "Maybe not, but I know how good it feels."

"There's a song, goes . . . something . . . something, you and me against the world." Marge sang a snatch of the tune. "That's kind of the way I feel right now." She clasped her hands around her knee and rocked back on her spine. "But let me tell you, I'm not ready for the empty-nest syndrome. Half a nest is better than no nest at all."

Trish turned on her side and reached out with one hand to stroke her mother's hands. "So I'm half a nest, am I?"

"We've got a lot ahead of us, Tee." Marge's voice wavered.

"Sometimes it scares me. I mean, like this is my last year in high school. And I want to do so many things in the racing world too. How am I gonna do it all?"

"Well, one thing I've been learning is that I have to make choices. So I pray and ask God to help me make the right choices. Then I do what seems best. Remember what your father always said: 'The right choice always follows God's principles, and then you pray for God to close the doors He doesn't want you to go through.'" She paused and wiped away a tear that trickled down her cheek. "It helps to talk about him, you know."

"I think I finally can." Trish sniffed and reached for a tissue. "I still feel like a yo-yo sometimes. And I never know when it will happen."

"Me too. But thank God, we've got each other." Marge leaned forward and kissed Trish on the cheek. "Good-night, Tee. You and Rhonda will knock 'em dead tomorrow."

After saying her prayers with lots of things to be thankful for, Trish snuggled down under the covers. What a day this had been!

The alarm rang after Trish had already headed for the bathroom. The beep, beep, beep met her when she returned. She thumped it off and dressed quickly. When she stood in front of the full-length mirror, she couldn't keep from smiling. Who was that person?

Marge walked up behind her. "Wow. You're all grown up. Trish, you look beautiful." She stroked the waves of glossy, midnight hair that swung just past Trish's shoulders. "I haven't seen you with your hair down for so long, I forgot how rich it is." She touched the dangly turquoise-and-bead earrings. "The whole outfit fits together so perfectly." She gave Trish a quick hug. "Breakfast's ready. I had cinnamon rolls in the freezer, so you get the royal send-off."

"What, no bagels?" Trish slipped an arm through her mother's. "Lead me to 'em."

A few minutes later Trish stepped out into the sunshine. "You sure you don't need your car today?"

"Nope. I'm home to stay. I'll drive you if I need it any other day this week or use the pickup." Marge stood in the door and waved. "Of course, you could take the bus."

Trish flipped a grin and a wave over her shoulder. She was spoiled, she knew it. The last three years, first David, then Brad drove. And this year she would have her own car when she brought it back from California.

She waved again as she drove down the driveway. Her senior year was about to begin.

She picked up Rhonda, who wore her wild red hair confined in a braid and finished with a broad ribbon. Their outfits matched except for Rhonda's turquoise blouse and darker denim skirt.

"Welcome home and don't we look like something out of a magazine ad? My mom can't get over the difference." She swung up in the van and dumped her purse and book bag on the floor. "I don't think I'm ready to dress like this all the time, though. Takes too much time."

"Me too. Bad as polishing boots and goggles before a race." Trish checked both ways before pulling out on the road. "Hey, you want to fly to California on Friday? That way I'll have someone to ride back with me."

"I'll ask. Sounds like fun."

A few minutes later, Trish chewed her bottom lip

while she drove up and down the lot at the high school, looking for a place to park. Last year had been a rough one. What did this year hold?

Football quarterback Doug Ramstead waved her into a parking place beside his shiny black pickup with red flames painted on the side. "Good to see ya, Trish, Rhonda." He clapped a hand to his forehead. "Oh, wow! You two are . . ." A wolf whistle came from another car.

Rhonda and Trish grinned at each other as they strolled across the parking lot. Yep, that was the reaction they wanted.

"Maybe he still likes you." Rhonda nudged Trish and glanced toward the blond, biceps-bulging football star. "He did last year."

CHAPTER FIVE

"I think this is gonna be a fun year." Rhonda slid into the seat next to Trish. Fourth-period government was the only class they had together.

"What makes you think that?" Trish dug in her purse for a lipstick. She ducked her head to peek into the narrow mirror attached to the lipstick tube. After applying a coat of cranberry lip gloss, she rolled her lips together and put everything back in her purse. She straightened just as the teacher, Ms. Wainwright, entered the room.

"She's new," Rhonda whispered. "She's the drama coach too."

"I know, I have her for speech seventh period," Trish answered.

The final bell rang. Trish caught a movement out of her eye. She turned her head to see Doug Ramstead take the seat on her other side. He grinned at her and waved at Rhonda.

"From now on, you will all be in your seats by the final bell." The teacher stood in front of the class, looking more like one of the students than a faculty member. Her wavy blond hair, caught up in combs on the sides, tumbled below her shoulders. Wire-rimmed glasses failed to hide the twinkle in her blue eyes, even though her words sounded stern.

Trish heard a faint whistle from somewhere behind her. He was right. Their new teacher could make plenty of money modeling in her spare time.

"As you can see on the board, my name is Carolyn Wainwright, and due to the school policies, you'll be wise to call me Ms. Wainwright. You may have heard, I am also the new drama coach, and I'll see some of you in speech this afternoon.

"Now I know you all groan at the thought of a semester on how our country is governed, but I guarantee you'll understand the process better by the time we're finished. As our preamble says, this is government 'of the people, by the people, and for the people.' Since many of you will be eligible to vote in the next election, we'll start with local government and politics. By the way, there'll be ways to earn extra points for outside activities."

Trish listened carefully. The teacher's enthusiasm overrode even the rumbling of a hungry stomach. Trish rubbed her midsection and hoped no one could hear the noise.

"Me too," Doug Ramstead whispered.

Trish could feel the heat begin at the base of her neck. Rhonda giggled on the other side of her. Trish shot a glare at her friend and tried to ignore the blush she knew stained her cheeks by now. She felt like using the papers in her notebook to fan her flaming face.

When the bell rang, she joined the rush for the door.

"What a babe."

Trish heard two guys talking behind her.

"Yeah, and to think she's a teacher. What a waste."

Trish glanced at Rhonda, and the two rolled their eyes upward in the age-old feminine sign of disgust for crude comments. Especially such comments from those of the male gender.

"So, how's our world-class jockey doing?" Doug Ramstead inserted himself between them with an arm about each of their waists. "You two starting a new rage at good old Prairie?"

"Meaning?" Rhonda shifted her books to her other arm.

"Such hot threads." He grinned at Trish. "Being a world-class jockey must be paying off."

"Thanks, I think," Trish answered.

"How about eating lunch at my table?"

"Your table!" Rhonda pulled open the door, only to have him reach over her and hold the door for both of them. "Who died and made you king?"

"He thinks being the big QB gives him special rights. Like there's a table in there labeled *football stars*." Trish turned to leave her stuff in her locker.

"I'll save your places," Doug said over his shoulder.

"Did that all just happen or have I been caught in a dream warp?" Rhonda leaned against the closed locker next to them and fanned her face.

"You nut. He's just Doug, same as he's always been."

"Yeah, a flirt, gorgeous, *the* quarterback of Prairie High, and he liked our outfits."

"Who wouldn't?" The girl with the locker next to them interrupted. "Where'd you find clothes like that?"

"California." Rhonda assumed a model's languid pose against the lockers. She ruined it with a giggle.

"You still racing?" The girl asked Trish.

"Yeah, but now only on weekends. Depends on when Portland Meadows opens." The three made their way toward the lunchroom.

58

"You sure did well. I kept reading about you and Spitfire winning the Triple Crown. That was really something." She tucked her long straight hair behind her right ear.

"Thanks. Seems like it all happened so long ago."

"Over here." Doug Ramstead waved from the table Brad, Rhonda, and Trish had always sat at.

Trish and Rhonda exchanged glances. Rhonda shrugged and raised her eyebrows. "This is gonna be fun," she whispered as together they carried their trays with salad, milk, and rolls across the room, dodging bodies and trays as they went.

"Sit here." Doug patted the seats beside him on his left. "I beat off those meatheads for you."

By the time they finished lunch, Trish felt like she'd returned to a world she'd nearly forgotten. It seemed as if her life at the track and her life at home were in two different galaxies, at least a time warp apart.

"I think he likes you," Rhonda said just before they separated to go to their classes.

"Right. He invited us both, remember?"

"Yeah, but he *likes* you."

"And I like a jockey."

"Who's in Kentucky."

"Rhonda, go to class." Trish stepped into her classroom just as the bell rang.

By the end of the day, she felt like if she had to sit still one more minute, she would fly into bitty pieces. What a difference between tracktime and schooltime. During the last minutes before the bell rang, she pictured what she would be doing at the track. Most likely waiting in the jockey room or riding in a race, the horse driving for the finish line.

Her mind flashed to Kentucky. *Wonder what it would take to bring Red out to the tracks on the West Coast?* she thought. What if she could see him more often? Her middle turned to mush.

The bell rang, sending her dream into a billion splinters.

She caught the end of the teacher's statement. Something about bringing gear for the weight-training class.

She stopped one of the other students. "What did he say at the end?"

"Bring your gear tomorrow."

"I know, but what gear specifically?"

The boy looked at her like she'd slipped a cog somewhere. "Like gloves, sweats or shorts, you know." He stared at her a moment more. "Say, you're Trish, the jockey, aren't you? How come you need weight training? Don't you get enough of a workout at the track?"

Trish fell into step beside him. "Nope, not right now. Especially not since Portland Meadows might not be opening."

"What are you going to do?"

Trish shrugged. "Beats me. There's a meeting tonight about it."

"Well, good luck." He paused before turning off to his locker. "See you tomorrow?"

Trish nodded. "All ready for a workout." After dropping off her books at her locker, Trish headed for the van. The boy's question drummed in her ears. What *was* she going to do?

Nagger uncurled from his prolonged nap and whispered in her ear, *Nothing, if your mother can help it. And remember, you don't want to get on her bad side again.*

This new peace between the two of you has been pretty nice.

Trish answered a couple of greetings as she crossed the parking lot, but she didn't slow her step. She and Patrick had plenty of work to do. And today she would see her long-time friend, Brad Williams. No, Clark College hadn't started yet. Funny, she didn't know his schedule either. She had lots of catching up to do.

Rhonda waited for her beside the maroon minivan. A guy tall enough to make her look short leaned against the van door, occupying all the redhead's attention.

Trish stopped a bit away. Rhonda sure was getting the looks today. Who was this guy? Certainly a new man on campus. And one who looked like he'd already made himself at home.

"Hi." Trish unlocked her door and threw her book bag on the floor between the seats. She hit the automatic unlock button on the door so Rhonda could get in.

"See ya." Rhonda followed Trish's actions and slid into the seat. "Cool dude, huh?" She waved just before slamming the door.

"Who is he?" Trish put the key in the ignition.

"Jason Wollensvaldt. Our exchange student from Germany. Would you believe I met him in German class?" Rhonda's words tripped over themselves in her rush to give Trish the news.

"Why's he taking German if he's from there?" Trish followed the line of vehicles out the side gate of the parking lot onto 117th Avenue.

"Telling us about life in Germany. He's planning to play basketball."

"I'm sure by tomorrow you'll know his life history."

"Maybe. He said he was going to call me this evening."

"Fast work, Seaboldt." Trish shook her head. "Hope he likes horses."

Even the van seemed to take a deep breath to recover from Rhonda's nonstop enthusiasm after she had made her exit. Trish waved in return and sucked in the silence. Rhonda thought school would be fantastic this year. Trish wasn't ready to concede fantastic, but things were looking mighty good. Doug Ramstead seemed determined to spend more time with them. Or was it her? She mentally shrugged. Didn't hurt to be invited to sit at the same lunch table as the most popular guy at Prairie High.

The baby blue Mustang occupied its normal place in the driveway. Brad would be either down helping Patrick or in the kitchen making sure the latest batch of cookies didn't go to waste.

Trish stepped out of the van with ladylike precision, simply because with a long, straight skirt, jumping wasn't possible. She leaned forward to accept a doggie kiss, and after ruffling Caesar's ears, entered the front door.

Chocolate-chip-cookie perfume greeted her nose even before the sound of voices announced her mother's whereabouts. Trish dropped her bag on the counter, picked up two cookies, still warm from the oven, and ambled into the dining room where Brad, Patrick, and Marge sat around the table.

"Look at you." Brad accompanied his comment with a wolf whistle, a difficult accomplishment with a mouthful of cookie.

"Thanks, I guess." Trish patted his head as she

walked by him to her place at the end of the table. "Hi, Patrick."

"How was school?" Marge handed around a napkin.

"You should ask Rhonda. I think she's in love."

"Already?" Marge leaned back in her chair. "Other than that, how was your day?"

"I think this'll be a good year. New drama coach. I have her for American Government and speech. She says we each need a special project. Plus a term paper, plus a couple of shorter papers." She copied her mother's laid-back pose. "Nothing much to keep me busy."

Brad leaned over and snitched the cookie she'd laid on the table. "Be glad you're not in college yet. They think term paper means once a week." Trish groaned along with him and made a grab for her cookie. "Hey, pig face, that's mine."

"Now children, there's plenty more where that came from."

Brad grinned around a mouthful of crunch. "David told me to keep you on your toes while he was gone. Afraid you'd get soft or something without a big brother to keep you in line."

Trish snorted in mock disgust. "Dream on."

"Well, how about the two of you joining me at the stables before you come to blows." Patrick pushed his chair back and picked up his battered fedora. "Thanks for the coffee." He stopped at the sliding glass door. "You coming down too, Marge? We need to be showin' these young hotshots how much you've done with the babies."

Marge nodded. "I have to return a phone call, so Trish and I'll be down in a few minutes."

"Who was that?" Trish asked after changing her clothes.

"Bob Diablo. Reminding us about the meeting to-night. Said to tell you 'buenos dias' and he's glad you're home again."

"So we're all going?" Trish shoved Caesar with her knee so he could tear around and bark at her. His tongue lolled to one side in a doggie grin of delight.

"Unless you have homework."

"Right."

After galloping the three horses Patrick was training for outside owners, Trish leaned on the paddock fence and watched her mother lunge Miss Tee. The filly half reared and struck out at an imaginary foe with her front legs. At a twitch of the line, she settled back to a spirited trot, her lengthening brush of a mane bouncing in the breeze.

"Hard to believe she's really a year old." Trish rested her elbows on the fence.

"We'll start with a saddle and pad soon. The gelding Feelin' Free is ready for breaking." Patrick watched the action with a smile on his face. "Your mother has come a long way."

"Yep. Makes me jealous that Miss Tee knows her better than me."

"True, for now. But that'll change when you start riding her." Patrick turned to look directly at Trish. "Caring for the babies filled a big hole in your mother's life. She gets terrible lonesome sometimes."

"She tell you that?" Trish turned her head to look at him with surprise.

Patrick shook his head. "Didn't need to."

Trish studied her mother. Graying hair feathered back on the sides, and one lock flopping down on her forehead, Marge looked years younger than forty. Her full mouth curved in a smile as the filly shook her head. Booted feet spread to brace against any coltish behavior, and her plaid shirt rolled up to the elbows, Trish's mother looked totally relaxed and competent.

Why, she's beautiful, Trish thought. *And she's having a great time.* Trish shook her head. All those years when Hal had been alive, Marge had never worked with the horses. In fact, Trish thought her mother hated or at least disliked the animals. Maybe this was another of those things she'd have to rethink. Could they work together?

———

That night the three of them rode to the racetrack in the minivan. Trish sat in the back, thinking about the meeting ahead. This was another first for her, the first TBA, Thoroughbred Association, meeting without her father. He'd been president of the organization several times through the years.

With a rush the tears stung the backs of her eyelids and clogged her nose. Trish sniffed and dug in her purse for a tissue. Before she could roll her eyes in evasive action, the drops trickled down her cheeks. She blew her nose and mopped her face.

Marge reached back with one hand and patted her daughter's knee.

Trish sniffed again. When she took a deep breath, it was as if a storm had crackled with heat lightning and then blown over after smattering the earth with only a drop or two. "Whew." She let her air out on a sigh. With one finger she wiped beneath her eyes to keep her mascara from smudging. At least she wouldn't go into the meeting looking like a raccoon.

It seemed like years since she'd been at Portland Meadows. The lighted horses that usually raced across the front of the dark green building were only dim outlines. Vehicles filled the parking slots closest to the building. It didn't look to be a large crowd.

Trish walked through the glass doors along with her mother and Patrick. Her father should be here. He'd know what to do. She swallowed the thought and clamped her jaw against the quiver she could feel returning.

"Good to see you Trish." Someone called from the group of men congregating in the corner. "Welcome home," another voice added.

"Thanks." Trish tossed the word in that direction along with an almost smile.

"You all think you could get in here so we can start this meeting?" Robert Diego poked his head out of the door. "Buenos dias, amiga." His dark eyes crinkled at the corners when he saw Trish. Even his mustache smiled. "Welcome home."

Trish stilled the quiver enough to return his greeting. As the members filed into the room, she started toward a chair at the back.

"Mind if I sit here?" A man wearing a brown leather bomber jacket pointed at the chair beside her.

Trish looked up into smiling hazel eyes. "No, I guess not."

"My name is Curt Donovan. I'm from *The Oregonian*." He took off his jacket and hung it over the back of the tan folding chair.

"I'm Trish Evanston."

"I know. I've been writing about you for months. Not often a reporter gets to be in on history." He sat down on the chair and turned to watch her.

"History?" Trish felt like she was reacting in slow motion.

"You set records. First woman to win the Derby. First woman to win the Triple Crown. Congratulations."

"Oh, that." Trish blinked. It seemed like that had all happened in another lifetime. "Umm, thanks." She dug deep for her manners, aware that her mother sat on her right.

A gavel rapped from the podium. "Let's call this meeting to order."

Trish thought a moment and then asked the questions that had been plaguing her. She spoke in an undertone so as not to disrupt the meeting. "Curt?"

"What?" He leaned close to hear her.

She turned her head, keeping one eye on the speaker. "Do you think . . ." She stopped to listen as Bob Diego called for a report from the secretary. "Have you heard anything, you know, illegal or something going on here at the track?"

Marge put a finger up to her lips and shook her head. Trish leaned close to hear Curt's answer.

"No, have you?"

Trish nodded and watched her mother out of the corner of her eye. "Sort of."

"We'll talk later."

Trish could feel her mother's frown clear down to her bones.

CHAPTER SIX

"I thought I asked you to stay out of that." Marge laid her purse on the counter with extreme care.

Trish walked to the sink and filled a glass of water at the tap. "I just asked if he'd heard anything."

"And then you agreed to talk with him further." Marge crossed her arms across her chest. "Trish, I just don't want you to get involved."

"Mother, we are involved whether we want to be or not. If that track doesn't open, where will we race? I race." Trish put her hand to her chest. She fought against the catch in her voice. "You know how much I hate to have someone else ride our horses. That's my job."

"I know how . . ." Marge shook her head. "No, I don't know exactly how you feel, but I think I understand." She held up a hand to ward off Trish's protests. "I know you want to ride, especially after almost quitting, but things aren't the same as they used to be. No one else could ride Spitfire. You had to be there. But now others can ride for us, and if we have to, that's what we'll do."

Trish felt an angry fist grab her gut and twist. She stared at the square set of her mother's chin, then clamped her arms across her belly to halt the twisting.

"Why are you being so unreasonable?" She fought to keep her voice from rising to a screech. If only she could scream and yell. "I don't want someone else to ride our horses."

Go ahead, act like a little kid again and then she'll really think you're ready to be treated like an adult. Nagger was only voicing the words she'd been burying.

Marge turned and leaned her weight on her rigid arms, staring out the window at the mercury-lighted yard. "I think I'm being very reasonable. All I'm asking is that you stay out of the controversy—if there really is one—at Portland Meadows."

"But somebody has to be involved."

"Somebody is. You heard them vote to ask for an extension before the city council votes. Bob Diego will take the petition to the council tomorrow night."

"Sure, after they argued back and forth. They're scared to do anything. You'd think they want the track to close. What a bunch a . . ." She sucked in a deep breath and adopted a more controlled tone. "All I want is to be able go to the meetings and see what happens. That isn't too much to ask."

"Trish, we'll talk about this later." Bright red stained Marge's cheeks, and her voice snicked each word like a scalpel.

Trish stared at her mother. Angry words threatened to pour past her clenched teeth, but instead of spitting them out, she turned and stormed down the hall to her room. This was such a stupid fight. She grabbed the edge of the door, ready to slam it closed, but stopped. The click sounded even louder than her pounding heart.

All the things she wished she'd said thundered through her mind as she undressed for bed. She threw her jeans in the corner and flung her shirt over the back of the chair. Why bother to put things away? Just because her mother liked a clean room. She barely resisted kicking the chair leg when she nudged it with her stockinged toe.

"If you really cared about my riding, you'd let me go," she muttered to herself as she pulled her nightshirt over her head. "You never wanted me to ride anyway." The box of tissues fell to the floor when she snapped off the lamp on her bedstand. The name she called it wouldn't fit in Sunday school.

When Trish curled up under the covers, she shivered in her fight against the tears. Here she'd only been home a few days, and she and her mother were already fighting. *It's not fair. She just doesn't understand.*

Yeah, sure, you think you're so grown-up, and here you are fighting again. Thought you promised not to lose your temper anymore. The voices raged inside her head.

If you controlled your temper better. If Mom only cared enough about me and the horses. She doesn't understand. What if I have to quit riding. I can't stand all this. I hate being mad.

She turned over and fumbled on the floor for the tissue box. After blowing her nose—again—she flopped back on the bed and let the tears trickle down into her ears. The yawning pit reached up with tentacle arms to suck her down in.

At the thought of saying her prayers, she blew her nose again and turned over. Sure, ask God for help. How could she when she knew He'd expect her to go and tell her mother how sorry she was. Sorry was right. What a sorry mess.

The nightmares returned with a vengeance. Trish

awoke sometime in the night with her heart pounding like she'd run two miles. A weight seemed to sit on her chest, threatening to cut off the air she gulped as if it were nearly gone.

When she tried to picture Jesus in her mind, all she could see was her mother's eyes. Sad eyes with a hint of a tear at the corners. Angry eyes too, with sparks that flashed when the two of them got into it.

Trish scrubbed her hands across her own eyes. She had promised herself to never fight with her mother again. They didn't need it, either of them. A sense of desolation settled over Trish's bed, pushing her heart down through her ribs and into the bedsprings. It lay there, heavy and thick, clogging her throat and burning her eyes.

When she finally fell asleep again, it was to toss and turn, trying to throw off the suffocating blanket.

When she awoke, she knew she should go ask her mother's forgiveness. It was the only thing to do. But when she entered the kitchen ready for school, the emptiness echoed around her. The full coffeepot told her that Marge had been there. Trish walked back through the living room and checked her mother's bedroom. Empty. In the living room, she stopped to stare at her father's recliner. If only he were here, life would be so different. Back in the kitchen, Trish looked out the window. The van stood dripping in the misting rain. So her mother hadn't left the farm anyway.

Trish sucked in a deep breath that only went as far as the top of her lungs. The weight wouldn't let it go any further. So her mother was down at the barn. She probably had plenty to do down there. So what?

After fixing herself a slice of peanut butter toast and

pouring a glass of milk, Trish meandered back to her bedroom, munching as she went. If only she could talk with her mother the way she had with her father. He understood. And he wasn't a worrywart. She shook her head and blinked her eyes. If she started crying now, her mascara would run and she'd have to do her makeup all over again.

She grabbed her book bag and purse, retrieved the empty glass from her desk, and headed for the front door. The urge to throw the glass into the sink surprisingly changed into rinsing it out and sticking it in the dishwasher. At least she couldn't be accused of leaving the kitchen in a mess.

She headed out the door for the van. If only she had her own car, then she wouldn't have to use her mother's. She tossed her bags in the center and buckled her seat belt. What a lousy, rotten day this looked to be. And all because her mother lived at the height of unreasonableness. If she'd dared, she'd have spun gravel on the way out.

She turned into Rhonda's driveway. Maybe she should go live with the Finleys. They seemed to know what a kid needed.

"Hi." Rhonda leaped into the van, shaking her head to keep the raindrops from sinking into her fly-away mass of carrot waves and curls. She took one look at Trish's face. "Uh-oh. What's wrong now?"

"You don't want to know." Trish put the van in motion before Rhonda finished settling into the seat.

"Probably not, but tell me anyway. That way I know when to duck."

"Yeah, well." Trish clamped her teeth on her lower lip. If she talked about it anymore, she'd cry. And she was *not* going to cry over a fight with her mother or anything else.

After the silence lengthened, Rhonda turned to her friend. "Let me guess then. You had a fight with your mom."

Trish shot her a surprised glance. "How'd you figure that out?"

"Easy. No one else to fight with at your house, and you're wearing your don't-mess-with-me look."

Trish muttered something under her breath.

"Well?"

"Well what?" Trish waited for traffic to pass and turned into the Prairie High parking lot.

"What happened?" Rhonda enunciated carefully as if Trish were hard of hearing.

"She's telling me not to get involved with this mess at Portland Meadows."

"So."

"So what?"

"So, are you involved? And what does she mean?"

Trish parked the van by the back fence. "You know we went to the TBA meeting last night." Rhonda nodded. "I met a reporter there, Curt Donovan, from *The Oregonian*, and he got all interested when I asked him if he'd heard about anything wrong going on over there. Said he'd call me."

"Is he cute?"

"Rhonda Seaboldt, for Pete's sake, you got guys on the mind all the time?"

Rhonda rolled her eyes and shook her head. "No, dummy, but face it, if you're gonna be working with this Curt guy, you'll have more fun if he's cute."

Trish shoved her door open. "Forget it." She grabbed

her gear and stepped down, locking the doors in the same motion.

Rhonda fell into step beside her as they crossed the parking lot, trying to dodge between the raindrops. "Face it, now you're not so bummed out about your mom, are you?"

Trish just glared at her. Bummed out fit the bill, all right.

The drippy rain hadn't let up and neither had her mood by the time Trish returned home that afternoon. Sure she'd laughed and joked with the guys at the lunch table, but she could have been someone else for all she cared. She let Rhonda talk nonstop all the way home about Jason, the exchange student. That way she didn't have to answer any questions.

The truck was gone when she got home—and so was her mother.

After changing into her work clothes, Trish grabbed an apple from the bowl on the table and walked past the bubbling fish tank and into the living room. As if drawn by a magnet, she sank into the comforting arms of her father's recliner. When she closed her eyes and tipped her head against the cushiony back, thoughts chased each other through her mind. She needed to talk to her mother—that was a sure thing. She wished she could talk with her dad—that was impossible. And talking to God—why bother?

If she opened her eyes, Trish knew she would see that old black pit yawning before her.

You'd think you'd have learned all this by now. Nagger took this moment to come out of hiding. *You know we've been over and over this.* Trish laid her arm across her eyes.

Yeah. She thought she'd learned the lessons too. But it was so hard to praise God when things were in such a mess again.

"And I had such good intentions." She opened her eyes and let her gaze drift around the room. . . . The fieldstone fireplace where they'd toasted marshmallows and burned hot dogs. Her mother's rocking chair. Trish's gaze skittered past that item. Her father's Bible on the end table beside the chair.

It was as if he could come back at any moment; everything was waiting for him. She closed her eyes again. *She* was waiting for him. Before the burning could swell into tears, she pushed herself to her feet and headed for the barn. At least down there she wouldn't have time to think.

"Hi, Patrick, sorry I'm late." Trish pasted an almost smile on her face. It was the best she could do. And she didn't look the trainer in the eye.

"Not to worry." Patrick brought out the saddle and settled it just behind the gelding's withers.

"Where's Brad?" Trish fetched her helmet from the tack room.

"Had some errands to run before work today. He should be along any minute." Patrick checked the girth and cupped his hands to give her a leg up. "You want to tell me what's wrong now or later?"

Trish paused with her knee in the air. "How'd you know?" Patrick just shook his head and tossed her into the saddle. Trish stared down at the top of his grungy fedora. "Mom and I had a big fight."

Patrick nodded his head. "Sure and she's hurtin' too."

"She tell you?"

This time the old trainer shook his head. He looked up at Trish, laying his hand on her knee. "No. Just these old eyes see more'n I want them to sometimes."

"She said I had to stay out of the mess at The Meadows." Trish stroked her mount's black mane and down his shoulder.

"And yer sure there's something wrong there, then?"

"I don't know. What do you think? What have you heard?"

"I think you should walk this son once around and then gallop him nice and easy for another two." He took hold of the reins and turned the bay gelding toward the fenced oval. "Be watchin' him for any weakness in that right fore."

Trish started to say something but thought the better of it and nudged her mount forward instead.

"So what do you think I should do?" Trish asked when they'd finished the schedule Patrick had set. Brad had left for the day and no lights showed at the house yet.

"I think you know what to do. Your mother has good reasons for what she asks. The two of you will work something out."

Trish shut the tack room door and shoved home the latch. "What have you heard?"

Patrick shook his head. "I'm thinkin' I shouldn't be tellin' you this, but I know you'll hear it somewhere. A couple of bug boys were laughing about how Smithson, the assistant manager, must have won the lottery or something."

"The lottery?"

"He's driving a brand-new, loaded Corvette XR1. Cherry red."

"Smithson?"

"Now it may be that his uncle died and left him money..."

"Or he's in debt to his armpits."

"So I'm just a'tellin' you what I heard."

"Thanks, Patrick." Trish whistled for Caesar and trotted past Patrick's mobile home up to the house. She had homework to do, and maybe she'd put dinner in the oven.

"How come a house can feel and even smell empty?" she asked Caesar after sliding open the glass door to the deck. "Yes, you can come in." A quick yip and a doggie grin was her thanks.

Trish turned on the lights, retrieved a frozen casserole from the freezer out in the garage, and slid it into the heating oven. The collie padded behind her down the hall to her room and curled up on the rug by her bed. She was on the second chapter in her American Government book when she heard the truck return.

Trish's gaze locked on a card on the wall. "I can do all things through Christ who strengthens me." That one was in her handwriting. She muttered the verse for a second time before shoving the chair back. This wouldn't be easy.

"Mom, I'm sorry—"

"Tee, we have to talk." Their words mishmashed together into cords that drew the two of them into each other's arms.

Marge brushed Trish's bangs to the side and kissed her daughter's forehead. "I think I let the worries get to me again. I keep telling myself you're about grown-up, but something in me doesn't believe it."

"Where were you?"

"At my grief group, and then I stopped to talk with Pastor Mort. He said to remind you that the one for teens meets on Mondays at the Methodist church right after school."

Trish let that pass. "I hate fighting. Please forgive me?" She leaned her cheek against her mother's chest. Somehow the words weren't as hard to say as she'd feared.

"Of course." Marge leaned her cheek against her daughter's thick hair. She sniffed and dug in her pocket for a tissue. After blowing her nose, she sniffed again, this time in appreciation. "You started dinner. And here I was trying to figure out what we'd eat." She hugged Trish one last time. "How soon 'til it's ready?"

After dinner, Marge lit a fire in the fireplace and settled into her chair with her knitting. Trish brought her books in and curled up in her father's chair. Music drifted from the stereo, playing a countermelody to the snapping and hissing of the burning wood.

"We need to lay some ground rules for this year," Marge said when Trish closed her books.

"Okay." Trish felt a tug of resentment but reined it down.

"School has to be your first priority and good grades are—"

"Mom, I'll maintain a B or better, I promise."

"Thank you. I want you to be able to choose any college you want, and grades count." Marge leaned forward. "And no more than one road trip a month." The words fell into a shocked silence.

"But, but what if The Meadows doesn't open? I

can't—I need—M-o-t-h-e-r." Trish put all her pleading into that one word.

"We'll just have to deal with that when and if the time comes. Dad always said to take one day at a time, and that's what we'll do."

Trish leaned back in her chair. One road trip a month. Why, the trip to Kentucky would take care of October. And she was heading for San Francisco on Friday. So much for September. She raised her hands and then dropped them in her lap.

They *had* to get racing back at The Meadows. They just had to.

The ringing phone brought her to her feet. "I'll get it."

"Trish, I've decided to let you attend the city council meeting with me tomorrow night." Her mother tossed the comment at Trish as she passed.

Trish nearly lost her voice to the shock. "R-Runnin' On Farm," she stammered into the kitchen phone.

"Can I speak with Trish Evanston, please?" a strong male voice said in her ear.

"Speaking." The voice sounded familiar.

"Hi, this is Curt Donovan, the reporter from *The Oregonian*. You remember me?"

"Sure." Trish propped the phone between her shoulder and ear. "How can I help you?"

"I think I have some information you might be interested in."

Trish sank down to her corner, propped in the V of the cabinet and wall. "Really?"

CHAPTER SEVEN

"Can I meet with you after school tomorrow?"

Trish fumbled for an answer. "Ummm, I really don't have time. I start working with our horses here as soon as I get home from school."

"I could come there."

Trish thought hard. What if he had something important to ask her? Shouldn't she tell him what Patrick had said? He needed all the available information to conduct a decent investigation. "Just a minute, okay? I'll be right back."

She crossed her legs and rose to her feet. Placing the phone carefully on the counter, she walked back into the living room. "Mom?" Marge raised her head from counting stitches. "That's Curt Donovan on the phone. He'd like to come talk with me tomorrow after school."

"About Portland Meadows?"

Trish shrugged. "I guess." What else would he want to see her for? She kept her pose relaxed, nonchalant, like this didn't really mean much to her. Inside she was screaming *please, please!*

Marge laid her knitting in her lap. "If he comes, I want to be there, along with Patrick. And I need your promise that if I tell you to back out down the road, you'll do it without an argument."

Trish sucked in her breath. That was a tall order. "You mean . . ."

"I mean that Runnin' On Farm will do all we can to make sure there's racing at Portland Meadows this year, but we will do this together." She stared at her daughter, as if assessing Trish's honor. A hint of a smile tugged at the corners of her mouth. "After all, three heads are better than one." She picked up her knitting again. "And besides that, he's too old for you."

Trish felt the heat flame her cheeks. "Mother!" She fled to the kitchen, chased by her mother's chuckle.

After making the arrangements with Curt, she hung up the phone and ambled back into the living room. She shook her head at the question in her mother's eyebrows and settled back to finish her homework. Stranger things had happened, but at that moment, she was hard pressed to think of any.

———

Crossing the parking lot after school the next day, Rhonda pleaded for the chance to join the discussion.

"Oh, Rhonda. You just want to see what Curt looks like." Trish threw up her hands. "If I didn't know you better, I'd think guys took over your brain this summer."

"What's wrong with that? We're seniors, remember? We should have some guys in our lives. You have Red."

"Yeah, two thousand miles away." Trish flinched at the pang of guilt. She hadn't written to him since she'd come home. And she hadn't thanked the Shipsons yet either.

"Well, you could have Doug, too, if you'd open your eyes."

"Rhonda Seaboldt, you're the most . . ." Trish sputtered. She couldn't think of a name bad enough. At least not one that she would use on such a long-time friend and cohort.

Rhonda slammed the car door and pulled out her seat belt. "So, can I come?"

"Whatever." Trish started the car and joined the line of vehicles snaking out the back gate. "But if you . . ."

Rhonda raised one hand in pledge. "I'll keep a lid on this mouth of mine, I promise. Best friend's honor."

———

Trish carefully kept her gaze away from Rhonda after she'd introduced them. She knew she'd see that I-told-you-so expression. Curt Donovan wasn't just cute, he was good-looking. Dark blond hair, square jaw, and hazel eyes that lighted with laughter. All six feet of him announced an athletic past, if not present.

She would not look at Rhonda.

"So let me tell you what I've learned so far." Curt's deep voice brought her back to the moment. He raised his hands and shrugged. "Nothing."

Trish felt her stomach bounce down about her knees. She glanced at her mother, who raised an eyebrow. Patrick tipped his hat back and leaned against the board fence.

"Tell him what you heard." Trish nodded toward the trainer.

"Well, it ain't much. Just that Smithson, the assistant manager, is drivin' a fancy new Corvette."

"Really." Curt jotted something on his note pad.

"He drove a dented, chugging, rusted pickup before that," Trish added.

Curt raised an eyebrow. "Anything else?"

All three of them shook their heads.

"Except Mom's bad feeling."

Curt looked at Marge, who shook her head. "I have no basis for it in fact. Just that sometimes I have a feeling about things, and Hal always said to go with my gut."

Curt jotted down something else and stuck his paper back in his pocket. "Well, this gives me something to go on. Maybe I'll spend some time on the backside and keep my ears open. You hear anything else, you let me know, okay?"

"Will you be at the city council meeting tomorrow night?" Marge asked.

"Of course. I'll see you all then?" His question was for everyone, but his eyes asked Trish. At her nod, he smiled, said goodbye to them all, and strode back to his car. He waved just before climbing into the well-used compact.

"I think I'll go to the meeting too." Rhonda sighed.

"You nut." Trish gave her an elbow in the direction of her ribs. "Come on, you can ride Patrick's filly. I'll take the gelding."

When she got back to the house after chores were finished, a letter from Red lay on the oak table in the entry. "Fiddle." Trish slit the envelope and read the funny card as she walked down the hall. How come he always managed to write before she did? He must have mailed it from the airport just after they left.

Before she could get involved in anything else, she sat at her desk and wrote letters to both Red and the Shipsons. Thank you seemed such a weak word for all the charming couple had done for her and her mother.

Trish sealed the envelopes and took them down the hall with her. "You got any stamps?" She paused at the doorway of the kitchen to inhale. "What smells so good?"

Marge turned from checking something in the oven. "Sure. Stamps are in the desk like always and roast beef. How about mashed potatoes?"

"Great." Trish retrieved the stamps. After sticking them in place, she left the envelopes on the entry table so they'd get mailed. "Mom, I've been thinking."

"I'm glad."

"No, I mean really." Trish leaned a hip against the counter. "What could we send to the Shipsons as a thank-you gift? A card just doesn't seem enough."

"You're right." Marge poured herself a cup of coffee. "How about flowers?" Trish wrinkled her nose. "Candy." A shake of the head. "How about we give it some thought?"

"Okay." Trish rubbed a finger across her chin. It felt like a zit was starting. She headed for the bathroom and some medication. She stared at the face in the mirror, making faces to check her skin. Sure enough, another one by her nose. Must be close to that time of the month. Maybe that's why she'd been feeling like falling into the yawning pit.

She made another face at the girl in the mirror and flicked out the light. She had a speech to prepare for next week. What could she talk about?

Something you're grateful for. For a change Nagger tried to be helpful.

She was still thinking about it when she climbed into bed that night. One thing she was grateful for—no chemistry this year. Another thing, tonight she could say her prayers. Somehow when she was angry, like at her mother, praying didn't seem to work. *Maybe because you don't pray then.* Nagger honed in like a laser.

She remembered to ask for forgiveness along with the praises. The "please helps" included Portland Meadows. "Please, God, let the track open again. If there is a mess there, please clean it up. And take care of David. The house sure seems lonesome without him." Her last thought was that she should have sent him a card by now too. So much to do.

───────

She ignored Rhonda's teasing looks all the next day. But it wasn't hard. Her friend really had a friend, of the male variety. The tall exchange student sat at their table for lunch and hung out at their locker to walk Rhonda to class when he could.

"Is it okay?" Rhonda asked in an undertone after Jason invited her to go with him for a milkshake after school.

"Sure." Trish shoved the books she'd need into her bag and slammed their locker. "Have fun." But the drive home seemed long and lonely. Was this to be another change in her life? The thought didn't help lighten her mood any.

Patrick had Dan'l saddled when Trish got down to the barn. "What's happening?" Trish took a last bite from her apple and fed the core to Dan'l. The old gray thoroughbred crunched the treat, then nosed her pockets in the hopes of more. Trish scratched his favorite spot, right behind his ears, and stroked down his cheek while waiting for an answer.

"Thought we'd give these two a taste of real racing,

even though they haven't learned the gate yet." Patrick led out the filly, and Brad brought the gelding. "You take her there and Brad, you on the boy." Patrick gave the instructions after mounting Dan'l.

Trish and Brad exchanged grins. "Kinda like old times." Brad settled his mount down to a flat-footed walk. The gelding obeyed for only an instant before he sidestepped and jigged in place.

"Think you can handle him?" Trish stroked the docile filly's neck.

"Who'd you think's been working this joker while you were gone?" Brad tightened his reins again.

Trish massaged the inside of her cheek with her tongue. "Shame you didn't teach him better manners then." She heard Patrick's chuckle just behind her. Dan'l snorted and pranced up alongside her left. "Hey, old man, you're looking mighty fine."

"Thank you." Patrick tipped his hat with his whip.

"I meant the horse." Trish grinned to let him know she was teasing.

"Sure and ye'll be hurtin' an old man's feelin's."

"Right." Trish nudged her mount into a trot. "Once around and then let them out at the quarter pole, right, Patrick?" At his grunt, she let the filly extend her trot.

The sun in her face, the breeze ruffling her bangs even under the helmet, the grunt of good horseflesh, and time with her friends. What more could she ask for, Trish thought. She smashed the lid on the thought of her father riding Dan'l instead of Patrick.

When they neared the quarter pole, they broke into an easy gallop, lining three abreast and, at Patrick's signal, let the excited horses out.

Trish, on the rail, crouched over the filly's withers,

the horse's mane whipping her chin. "Come on, girl, we gotta do this fast. You can't let those other two past."

The filly lengthened her stride, running flat out and low to the ground. Her heavy grunts rang like music in Trish's ears.

Dan'l, in the middle, dropped back so the filly and gelding ran neck and neck. Inch by inch the filly pulled ahead. "We did it!" Trish stood in her stirrups and eased the filly back to a slow gallop. "We won! Good girl."

"Just because you weigh so much less." Brad kept pace with his mount. "This poor fella had to carry too much weight."

"Excuses, excuses." Trish flipped her goggles up and after sitting back in the saddle, patted the filly's dark neck. "Face it, girls are just better than guys, right girl?" The filly snorted and tossed her head.

Brad snorted too, but the sound carried a different meaning.

"Isn't that right, Patrick?" Trish threw a grin at the trainer when he trotted up to join them.

"Don't answer," Brad said. "She'll get the big head if you agree. Besides, we all know that men are better. That's why God created Adam first."

"Naa, He got it right on the second time. Practice makes perfect, you know."

By this time they were back at the barn.

"Children, children. You'll never solve that old quibble, so let it be." Marge stood with her hands on her hips, laughing up at them. "Sorry, Patrick. I tried to teach them correct biblical principles."

"You did fine with me, Mrs. E. Just that girl-child you messed up with." Brad ducked behind his horse when Trish faked a punch at him.

"How about if we all go out to dinner before the meeting?" Marge held the filly's reins while Trish stripped the saddle off. "You can eat with us and then go home if you'd rather not go to the council meeting, Brad."

"You think I'd miss that? No way." Brad brought buckets out with him so they could wash the horses down.

"How about pizza?" Trish heard Patrick's groan. "All right then, Mexican." A groan this time from Marge.

"Patrick likes good old American best." Brad cross-tied his horse and started sponging him down. "And not hamburgers."

"Steak it is." Marge picked up a sponge and started on the filly. "If we hurry, we'll get there before the crowd."

Between them, they had all three animals washed, scraped, and on the hot-walker in record time.

"You're getting pretty good at this horse stuff," Trish said as she and her mother walked up the rise to the house.

"Strange, isn't it? All those years I missed out on."

"You been riding yet?"

"Tee, give me a break. Training, washing, the business end—all that's in. Riding is definitely out. *You* can be queen of the saddle."

"You might really enjoy it. You know Dan'l could use more exercise." Trish shoved open the sliding door off the deck.

"Fine. We'll put him on the walker more often."

It is strange, Trish thought as she changed clothes. *Mom used to be almost afraid of the horses, and now look at her.* But when the picture of her father riding Dan'l galloped into her mind, she blacked it out immediately. Would she ever be able to think of him without crying?

———

Curt Donovan met them on the front steps of the city hall building. "He didn't win the lottery," he said after greeting them all and being introduced to Brad.

"No rich uncle, either?" Marge asked.

"No time to check that, but I'd sure like to see his bank account."

"Can you do that?" Trish turned in surprise.

"Not legally. We'd need a subpoena. But I can find out if he paid cash."

"How?" Trish let the others go through the door ahead of her.

"I have a friend at the dealership where he bought the car."

"How'd you know..."

"Checked the license plate, dummy," Brad chimed in. At Trish's questioning look, he shook his head. "You know, they all have their signs on either the plates or the surrounding frame."

"Oh." Trish shrugged. "That must be a guy thing, knowing stuff like that."

Brad shook his head again. "We've been having this discussion," he answered in response to Curt's questioning look.

"That's going to stop now. They've already started the meeting." Marge led the way through the door. They joined Bob Diego and several other thoroughbred breeders and trainers in the back rows.

After discussion raged on several other issues, the mayor finally announced the agenda item for Portland Meadows.

The topic had no more been introduced when one of the council members raised his hand. "I move we close the Portland Meadows Race Track, effective immediately."

Trish felt her jaw sag. Surely she hadn't heard him right!

CHAPTER EIGHT

"Don't panic. That's how the process starts," Curt whispered.

Trish let her breath out again, unaware she'd been holding it. "Good."

"Is there any discussion?" Mayor Bonnie Muldoon asked, then nodded at the presenting council member. "John."

The man shuffled some papers in front of him. "You all know that the track has been a problem for years, both financially and socially." He continued on with his comments, all in the negative. The five minutes seemed to stretch for an hour.

Trish felt like jumping to her feet and yelling back. Marge put her hand on her daughter's arm. Wasn't anyone going to speak for the track?

The man droned on. "And so you see, closing the track will not only cease to be a drain on city resources, we will be able to dispense with both a criminal and social problem with the transients out there."

Trish shut her mouth with a snap. What in the world was the idiot talking about? She turned to make a comment to her mother but again felt a restraining hand on her arm.

"We'll talk later," Marge whispered.

A current phrase flashed through Trish's mind: "Never let 'em see you sweat." She pasted herself to the back of the seat and forced her face to hide her thoughts, not telegraph them. Only by crossing her arms over her chest could she subdue the shaking.

Would no one defend horse racing in Portland?

Another council member raised his hand to talk. "Now I think we are getting the cart before the horse here," he said. "We race both thoroughbreds and quarter horses out there at the track, and I think we need to hear from some of those folks."

Trish breathed a sigh of relief.

Before the mayor could recognize Bob Diego, the man who spoke earlier began talking again. Trish read his nameplate: John Reimer.

"Why doesn't he be quiet?" Trish muttered under her breath.

She stared at the man talking. His dark three-piece suit stuck out from the other casual attire like a black sheep in a light flock. As she listened, his arguments made sense if one didn't know about life at the track and the people there. It made her want to gag.

Curt sat beside her, taking notes.

"Thank you, John," the mayor interrupted. "Mr. Diego, you wanted the floor?"

"Madam Mayor, I have here a petition from the Thoroughbred Association, asking for a delay in making the decision, called a continuance, I believe." Tall, dark, and with a commanding air, Diego spoke with a slight Spanish accent, his words carrying the same air of confidence he projected.

Trish felt like clapping. Talk about a good presentation; Diego had it.

The mayor looked down at her calendar. "Agreed. We will bring this issue to a vote in three weeks. That will give you time to present any reasons for not closing the track." Diego nodded.

"But Mayor, I showed you all we need to know." Reimer leaned forward. "There's no need for a continuance, I . . ."

The mayor slammed her gavel. "Next order of business."

When Trish looked back at Reimer, the daggers in his gaze pinned her to the seat. Chills snaked up her spine and out to her fingertips. The man was furious. But when she glanced to her mother and then back to the front, a mask had fallen in place . . . just like the daggers had never been there.

When the mayor announced an intermission, the TBA group gathered in the hall.

"So what happens now?" Marge asked the question Trish had on the tip of her tongue.

"Now we hire a lawyer and start preparing affidavits of fiscal and social responsibility." Bob Diego tapped the papers he carried against his other hand. "We have to convince them that keeping the track open is a sound business plan and good for the city of Portland. Not just for us."

"Mr. Diego, you heard Reimer's accusations about the problems at the track. What do you have to say?" Curt Donovan asked.

"I hate to hear anyone calling our people transients. They work too hard for that." A murmur of agreement ran through the group. "And his hinting at mafia or underworld connections, those innuendoes go along with all the racetracks, and it's just not true. At least not here."

"But there have been money problems out there?"

"They've had a hard time finding a good management company."

"Excuse me," Trish muttered to her mother. Without waiting for an answer, she strode after Mr. Reimer. This time her "excuse me" rang more loudly.

The man stopped and turned. "Yes?"

Trish hadn't realized how big he was until she stood toe to toe with him. "What is it you really have against Portland Meadows?" She forced her voice to remain calm.

"You heard me in the council room." As if playing to an audience, his voice expanded. "I pledged my support for a cleaner city, one without the riffraff around the track."

Trish narrowed her eyes. "I'm at the track a lot. Am I riffraff?"

"Now see here, young lady."

"The name's Trish Evanston. And without Portland Meadows I wouldn't have won the Triple Crown this year. I think you need to do some more research. Now, if you'll excuse me, I hate to take up any more of your valuable time." Trish spun on her heel and returned to her group.

"Bravo, Trish." Curt silently clapped his hands.

"You shouldn'ta done that." Patrick shook his head, his eyes sad.

Trish was sure if she turned around, she'd see the daggers again. With her back to the man, she could feel them. She didn't dare look at her mother.

By the time they walked out to the van, Trish felt as if she'd been riding a monster roller coaster—for an hour.

"But what can *we* do?" Trish slammed the van door after her.

"Attend the TBA meeting on Sunday." Marge turned the ignition. "And keep our mouths shut in public, at least until we know more."

Patrick buckled his seat belt. "What kind of business does that Reimer have?"

"He's a lawyer," Brad answered. "I asked one of the other council members."

"Figures." Trish rested her elbows on her knees. "I didn't like him much."

"Now that's an understatement if I ever heard one." Marge followed the arrows out to the I–5 freeway.

"What time is your flight tomorrow?" Brad asked.

"Seven, why?"

"I can take you over, if you want. Maybe Rhonda'd like to come too."

"I wish one of you would fly down with me so I wouldn't have to drive home alone."

"Sorry, gotta work for my dad tomorrow."

"Yeah, and Rhonda has a show tomorrow and Sunday. One of these days I'm going to get to watch her jump again." Trish hid a yawn behind one hand. "How about you, Patrick? You want a quick trip to sunny California? My treat."

"Don't do me no favors." Patrick tapped her knee with his hat. "Besides, I'm busy."

"You can take some time off, you know. Mother isn't that bad a slave driver."

"Thanks for the vote of confidence. Besides, Patrick

and I have something to do tomorrow."

"What?"

"There's a garden show at Washington Park. We have tickets."

"Oh." That's all Trish could think to say.

"And there's the TBA meeting on Sunday. You *do* want someone from Runnin' On there, don't you?" What could Trish say?

————————

Getting off the plane the next evening in California was like stepping into another world. Margaret greeted her with open arms.

"Oh, I've missed you so. Adam and I just rattle around in the condo without you there." She kept an arm about Trish's shoulders. "And how is your mother?"

Trish talked nonstop all the way home, bringing her "other" mother up-to-date on their adventures.

"And Spitfire remembered you?" Margaret asked questions whenever Trish took a breath.

"Boy, did he. I hated leaving him again." Trish patted away a yawn. "How's Adam?"

"You'll see in a minute. He said he'd wait up for us."

Walking into the condo felt about as comfortable as walking into her home in Vancouver. Trish set down her bag and gave Adam a hug.

"So, you're in trouble already, I hear?" Adam kept his hands on her upper arms and studied her face.

"What?"

"Trouble—can't keep you out of it, no matter how hard we all try."

Trish looked at Margaret, question marks all over her face.

"Don't tease her, dear. Can't you tell she has no idea what you're talking about?"

Trish felt like she'd just come in on a movie halfway through.

Adam dropped his hands and fished in his shirt pocket. He pulled out a folded paper and handed it to her.

"Patrick faxed this to me. I thought you'd already seen it."

Trish read the article through. "Well, I have to say he did a good job."

"You know this Donovan fellow?"

"Yep. He's nice. Told him all our suspicions about the track." She glanced back at the article. Third paragraph from the bottom talked about her confronting Reimer. She shrugged with a grin. "What can I say? The guy bugs me."

"He sounds like one of the movers and shakers."

"Yeah, the way he talked about the people at The Meadows, I wanted to move and shake *him*. According to Reimer, everyone out there is either a low-life transient or part of the mafia."

"So, from what the article says, TBA has three weeks to prove The Meadows is financially sound and should be supported?"

"Right." Trish shook her head. "Big order. 'Cause it's not, and we don't know why."

Before going to bed, Trish called home to let her mother know she'd arrived safely. Funny, how it seemed she lived in two separate worlds, one in Washington and the other here in California. Was she ready to be a truly professional jockey and travel all over the country, following the racing seasons? Maybe jetting around to ride certain horses? She snorted at her wonderings.

Not to worry. No one would fly her anywhere to ride with her lousy win record.

Trish shivered in the predawn chill. Trees and lamp-posts appeared to float on low-lying fog, the same fog that distorted both human and animal sounds, giving the track a spectral air.

"This would be fine for Halloween." Trish tried to bury her head in her jacket collar.

"Look at you, two weeks off and you've turned into a wimp."

"It's supposed to be warm in California, don't ya know?" When they rounded the corner to approach the Finley stalls, Firefly nickered immediately.

"See, she missed you." Adam waved at the bright sorrel filly. In the stall next to her, Gatesby hung his head over the gate and, trailing a mouthful of hay, tossed his head and nickered. "So did he."

"All he missed was my shoulder. Cut it out, you goof." Trish hung on to the gelding's halter to keep him from landing his famous nonverbal hello. She moved down the line, stroking and greeting each of the horses. Even their new addition, Gimmeyourheart, accepted her caresses.

When she reached the office, Adam handed her a whip and helmet. "Get up there and go to work and you'll warm up all right." Trish tucked the grip of the whip into her back pocket and raised her knee for the mount. "Just loosen him up. You're in the third with this old boy." Adam patted the gelding's neck. "Not been much for the winner's circle, but he's usually in the money. You two pushed the winner across the line last time."

"Yeah, maybe if we hadn't pushed so hard, we'da won." Trish tucked her gloved hands under her knees. "Hey, fella, at least you're warm." When Adam shook his head and tisked, Trish took up the reins and headed for the track.

In spite of her grousing, being back in the saddle felt mighty good. Bay Meadows felt more like home now than Portland Meadows. Fog and chill at both places. She smiled at the thought. But here the sun would be out soon, and the bustle told everyone there was racing ahead. Would that happen in Portland?

She forced her mind back to concentrate on the horse under her and those moving at paces from walk to breeze to flat-out. Her mount jigged sideways as they trotted counterclockwise around the outer edge of the track.

"Hey, Trish, welcome back!" One of the women jockeys waved when they met and passed. Another jockey saluted her with whip to his helmet. When Trish dismounted back at the barn, Juan's grin stretched across his face and back again.

Carlos boosted her aboard her next mount. "Good to have you back." Since he was never one to waste words, his greeting made her feel even more a part of the family.

"Gatesby been behavin' himself?" Trish asked.

"Right." Since Carlos's black eyebrows met his equally dark and shiny hair, the one word made up for many.

"You think he could make it at Golden Gate?"

"Possibly. If we don't knock him in the head first."

Trish's grin drew an answering one. "Don't eat all the bagels before I get done."

With works finished, Trish, Adam, and Carlos relaxed

in the office around the coffeepot and bagel box. "So, according to that article, something smells rotten in Portland." Carlos wiped the cream cheese off his mustache.

"Could be. Curt Donovan—he wrote that article—says he'll do some snooping. Who knows what good he can do, but let me tell you, that Reimer ticked me off from his first words."

"He's a lawyer, right?" Trish nodded. "Then who's he representing?" Adam sipped from his chipped "lucky mug."

Trish thought a moment. "He never said. He's a council member, though."

"Could be a conflict of interests there if he's tied up with anyone."

"Meaning?" Trish stopped chewing and stared at him.

"Well, he's supposed to look out for the good of the city, not any special interests, like TBA or . . ."

"He's not looking out for TBA, that's for sure."

"I know, that's just an example. Ya gotta keep an open mind."

"My mother wants me to keep my mind out of it, along with any other part of me that might get involved." Trish swigged her orange juice.

"She's right." Adam got up to pour himself another cup of coffee. "Anything going on here that I need to know about?" This question he directed at Carlos. "Good, then I have a meeting to attend. See you later."

Later for Trish was in the saddling paddock, preparing for the third race. "Now you just relax," Adam reminded her. "You both know what to do so give it your best."

Trish followed the pony rider out into bright sunlight. The clamor of the crowd, the blue of the sky, and the snapping flags over the infield combined to put her on top of the world. They paraded around the track and then back past the grandstand with Trish stiff-legged, high above the gelding's withers. He entered gate three like the pro he was and with no further ado, they were off.

Trish crouched tight against his mane, singing her song to his twitching ears. When she asked for more coming out of the second turn, he lengthened out and pounded after the two front-runners. Like an out-of-control express train, he bore down on and passed the horse running second. Stride by stride he ate up the length between them and the front-runner.

Trish could hear the crowd roaring. The two white pillars loomed ahead. Her mount grunted with each stride. Neck out, ears forward, he drew even, neck and neck. Nose to nose. And he was past. One length, two. He charged across the finish line like he won every race.

"Yahoo!" Trish pumped the air with the whip in her fist. "Thank you, God. What a way to start the day."

She tried to smile professionally for the picture but couldn't suppress the beaming. Winning felt so good.

"That's my girl." Adam and Martha flanked her, with Carlos holding the gelding's bridle. "See you again in the seventh."

Trish hustled back to change silks for her mount in the fourth. The trainer counseled her about keeping the filly back until the stretch because she had a tendency to run herself out too soon. This would be her first time at a mile.

Trish nodded and stroked the gray neck. Again the

crowd greeted the post parade with a roar. The filly acted as if the show was all for her benefit and walked into the gate like a pro.

A horse, two down, had to be gated twice, but then they were off. The poles whipped by. The filly decided to let Trish be the boss after the first turn and settled down to run. Which she did. She ran the others right into the dirt and won going away by four lengths.

Two wins in one day. This felt like old times at The Meadows back up in Portland, where Trish had won nearly half of her races.

After the ceremonies, Trish stopped her walk back to the jockey room when she heard a voice call her. She looked around to find the reporter who'd dubbed her "The Comeback Kid."

"Lookin' good there, Trish. How does it feel to be back in the winner's circle?"

"Good. Awesome good."

"Heard you were in Kentucky. You going to ride in the Breeder's Cup?"

"Who knows. I'm just glad to be riding today."

"You heard any more from Chrysler?"

"Nope, I think your sources are all wet. They use models in ads like that, not a kid like me." She waved a thanks at congratulations from someone in the crowd.

"I'll be the first to say I told you so. And good luck on the rest of your rides today. Sorry you're leaving California."

Trish looked after his retreating figure. How'd he know so much about her? And who were those sources of his? She shook hands with a young girl who offered her program for an autograph. After signing it, Trish answered what had become a pretty standard question:

"No, I don't get to race Spitfire again. And yes, you can try to be a jockey when you get older. Start by learning all you can about horses and riding right now."

By the time she got up to the jockey room, she needed a drink, and water wasn't enough. She headed for the pop machine, quarters in hand. She could hear a Diet Coke calling her name.

Her third mount quit running two furlongs from the finish line. It was all she could do to keep him going until the end.

Adam winked at her from his place by the fence. He met her by the walkway to the jockey rooms. "You think we should've put a claimer on that one?" Her snort made him laugh.

Her agent called to her before she went in. "Hey, Trish, I got a new one for you in the eighth, that okay?"

"Sure. How come?"

"Jockey came up sick. Think he has the Heidelberg flu."

Trish rolled her tongue across her teeth. The Heidelberg flu meant the jockey suffered from a hangover. She felt no sympathy at all for him.

"Glad to. I'm riding for Adam in the seventh. That makes five mounts today. Super!"

"Might as well go out with a bang." He shook her hand. "If I don't see you again before you leave, have a good trip. And I sure hope they race in Portland this year."

"Thanks. Me too."

Trish brought Adam's other horse in for a show. It was the filly's first stakes race, and Adam thumped her on the knee with joy. "You did good, kid."

And Trish agreed. She'd pulled the filly out of a tight

spot and felt grateful for the placing.

She mounted a rangy gelding for her final race. He met her with ears back and shook his head when the trainer secured the blinkers in place.

"Maybe we should scratch him," the trainer said in an undertone.

"Naw, he'll be fine," the owner insisted. "He just got up on the wrong side of the bed this morning." When the trainer tried to say something else, the burly owner cut him off.

Trish felt guilty for eavesdropping. But at this point, she wished the trainer had more guts.

The horse argued with the pony rider and half reared when the gatekeepers tried to lead him into slot five. Trish felt alarm leap from bone to bone up her spine.

"Come on, knothead." She forced the soothing tone into her voice. The horse shook his head. His back arched beneath her.

"Watch him." The gate assistant's warning was lost in the animal's shrill whinny.

CHAPTER NINE

"He's going over!"

Trish heard the warning as she felt the animal rise beneath her. As he went up, she pushed herself up and out of the irons. She threw herself at the round iron bars separating each horse. Anything to keep from being crushed against the rear gate by the brute she rode.

Pain shot through her left shoulder when she smacked against the rail. Hands grabbed her and hauled her up before she fell below the gelding's slashing feet.

It all happened so fast her heartbeat didn't catch up until she had her feet on the ground outside the gate.

Two of the keepers hung on to the horse where he stood shaking. "Got more than you bargained for, you old . . ." He called the horse a name not nearly bad enough in Trish's mind.

Like the horse, she couldn't stop shaking. Her left arm hung useless at her side. It felt like she'd struck her crazy bone, only instead of just the elbow, her arm screamed from shoulder to wrist. What would her mother say to this?

"You okay?" one of the men asked.

"All but my arm." Her teeth chattered between the words.

"Right. Let's get you outta here." He waved to the official. The gun sounded and the remaining field burst from the gates.

"I'm so sorry," the trainer apologized when he retrieved his horse. "I shoulda just did what I thought best."

Trish nodded. Her knees felt like cooked spaghetti, and they weren't the part of her that hurt.

"How about a hand getting over to first aid?" one of the gate men asked.

Trish nodded. Her chattering teeth let her know she was going into shock, so a warm arm to lean on sounded good. Adam met her at the fence.

"Thanks, I'll take her now." He wrapped an arm about Trish's waist and let her lean against him. "You want Carlos to carry you?"

Trish shook her head. "I can walk." She clutched her injured arm with the other, cradling it so the jolting didn't hurt so much.

"You think it's broken?" Adam pushed open the door to the first aid.

"Uh—uh." The thought of a broken arm sent her heart into overdrive.

"Let's have a look at that." The staff nurse sat Trish down in a chair and after closing the white curtain, unfastened her silks. The woman kept up a soothing monologue, not unlike Trish's own for spooky horses, while she examined the arm and shoulder.

"Good news. It's just dislocated. We can fix that in a jiffy." She stepped back to study Trish's face. "Now we can give you something for the pain first, but I'll tell you, the sooner we put it back where it belongs, the less inflammation we'll have. You tough enough for that?"

Trish nodded and bit her bottom lip. "Just do it."

"Would you rather wait for a doctor?"

"No."

The nurse called the masseur in to help. She explained what they had to do. "Now, you yell if you need to. We don't need any heroes here, okay?" Trish nodded again. Together they applied the right pressures and, on three, snapped the shoulder joint back in place.

"Ahhh!" Trish heard the grind and snap. Before she could say anymore, she could already feel the relief.

"We did it. Good job, Trish. You're a real trooper."

Trish panted out a "thank you." She accepted a glass of water along with a couple of pain killers. When she could breathe again, she forced a smile to her mouth. Licking her lips helped too.

"Okay, let's ice that sucker and then you can go home to bed. You don't have any mounts tomorrow, do you?"

"No, I'm driving to Vancouver early in the morning." Trish winced again when the nurse laid the blue plastic ice packets over the wet washcloths against her skin.

"You're what?" The nurse talked as she wrapped towels around the injury. Trish repeated herself. "That's what I thought you said. You get up here and lie down for a bit." She helped Trish climb up on a gurney and lie back. "Can't someone drive for you?" Trish shook her head. "Then wait a couple of days or fly."

"I wish." Trish closed her eyes. "I'll be fine. You said this was simple."

"True, but I didn't say it wouldn't hurt."

If only I'd left well enough alone, Trish thought as she

lay staring at the ceiling. *One more mount. I had to take one more mount.*

"Can I see her for a moment?" she heard Adam ask the nurse.

When she agreed, he pulled the curtain back enough to enter and leaned over the gurney. "How ya doing?"

Trish could feel her eyes fill at the concern in his voice. "Thank God it's not broken," she managed.

"What a bummer. They shoulda scratched that beast. Hank knows better than that."

"He tried. The owner wouldn't buy it." Trish turned her head so she could see him when he sat down in the chair by her bed.

Adam shook his head. "So now what are you going to do?"

Trish raised an eyebrow in question.

"About going home tomorrow."

"Drive. Why?" When she recognized the stubborn look on his face, she added. "I'll be fine, really I will. If I need to stop, I can do that. Adam, it was just dislocated. I'll wear the sling, and my shifting arm isn't injured."

"I'll drive you." He crossed his arms over his chest.

"No." She almost controlled the wince when she shook her head.

"Then Martha will. Or you'll fly."

"I have to get my car home." Trish blinked her eyes against the sleepiness caused by the pain pills. The warmth started at her feet and flowed upward. If she could just sleep awhile—

"Okay, Missy, let's get that sling in place and let you go home before this man paces a groove in my floor here." The nurse's voice called Trish back from the floating land of comfort.

Sitting up snapped her fully awake. "Ow."

"I know." The nurse adjusted the blue canvas sling and eased Trish's silks back in place, tucking the empty sleeve inside. She handed Trish two bottles with pills in them. "Now you take these to keep the swelling down and these will help the pain."

"Will they make me sleepy?"

"Most likely."

"Thank you." Trish stuffed the two small containers in her pocket. While she felt a bit woozy when she stood up, she ignored the feeling and nodded when Adam asked if she was ready. He had her bag from the jockey room in his hand. Trish thanked the nurse again and followed Adam out the door.

The sun setting behind the western hills told her how much time had passed since the accident. Trish got in the car carefully. She'd hoped to go out to the beach tonight. That's where she heard her song best, the one about eagle's wings. Boy, did she need eagle's wings right now.

That's where she'd finally found peace again and now she wouldn't even get to say goodbye. She leaned her head back against the headrest of the car seat. It would be so easy to blubber right now. She sniffed against the moisture pooling at the back of her nose and eyes.

But if she cried now, Adam would never let her drive tomorrow.

When Trish forced her bruised body out of bed in the

morning, a knock on her door announced Martha.

"How're you feeling?" She didn't wait for Trish's answer, instead handed her the blue ice packs. "Now you let this ice for a bit while I finish your packing for you. Then Adam will help load the car, and you and I'll be off."

"Martha, I'll be fine. You don't need to do this."

The older woman planted both fists on her rounded hips and stared at Trish, eyes narrowed. "If you think I'd let you go off by yourself injured like this . . ." She shook her head and turned back to the closet. "Why, your mother would kill me."

Not really, Trish thought, flexing her fingers. *She's going to want to kill* me! She knew she should have called home last night but—she rubbed her forehead with the uninjured hand. But she hadn't had the strength to argue and she *was* going to have her car at home.

"Don't even think about arguing with me." Margaret looked up from folding and packing Trish's things. "You know I'm right, and since your mother isn't going to be pleased about another injury, at least she'll applaud your good sense in allowing help."

What could Trish say? "Thank you" were the only words that came to mind.

She slept most of the eleven-hour trip home, waking only for food and rest stops.

"Those muscle relaxers appear to work pretty well," Martha said at one point when Trish rebuckled her seat belt.

At least it doesn't hurt as much this way, Trish thought as she dozed back to sleep again. Fighting to stay awake had already proven a wasted effort.

She woke up enough to direct Martha once they reached the southern edge of Portland. It didn't take long to get through the city and cross the Columbia River to Vancouver. Each mile closer to home brought increased alertness. Her heart picked up speed when they turned into the drive at Runnin' On Farm.

Caesar did his best to announce to the entire world that Trish was home again. Marge came out the front door as Trish stepped from the car. They met at the gate.

"How bad is it?" Marge checked her daughter over, looking for visible injuries.

"Just a dislocated shoulder. Margaret drove me up."

"Thank God." She squeezed Trish's good hand and walked on out to the car. "How good to see you. And thank you for caring for my kid there." The two women swapped hugs and retrieved the suitcases from the trunk and backseat. Burdened down, they made their way to the house.

Trish held the door for them. "At least I can do this one-handed." Her feeble attempt at a joke fell flat.

Marge set the things down and turned to her daughter. "Has it been X-rayed?" Trish shook her head. "Then I think our next order of business is to visit the emergency room and take care of that."

"Mother, the nurse said . . ."

"You haven't seen a doctor either?" At the look on Trish's face, Marge walked to her bedroom and returned carrying her purse. "Martha, if you'd like to kick back and relax for a while . . ."

"No, I'll go along. We can use the time to visit."

———————

Trish didn't dare say I told you so on the drive home again, but she sure wanted to. The doctor said exactly the same things the nurse had and approved the pills Trish was taking. Said she'd feel lots better in a day or two and the more she iced it, the better.

She didn't argue either in the morning when her mother prepared to drive her to school. The tight-lipped look her mother wore when helping Trish dress was enough to keep any thinking person silent, let alone a daughter who already felt guilty as charged.

"I'm sorry, Mom," Trish muttered. "It wasn't my fault."

"Tee, I know that. I'm not angry at you." Marge turned the ignition.

"Coulda fooled me." Trish buckled her seat belt with one hand. Having an injured arm wasn't easy, but she would not ask for help again.

Marge leaned her head on her hands. "It's just when something like this happens, I realize all over again what a dangerous sport you're—we're—in. You could be critically injured—or killed so easily."

Trish rolled her upper lip between her teeth. "But, you promised not to worry anymore."

"Yeah, well, the promise was easy. Livin' it ain't." She shot her daughter a watery grin. "It's only through the grace of God I keep my sanity at all. So . . ." She took a deep breath and let it out. "Thank God for His grace that can keep even a dyed-in-the-wool worrier like me under control. Times like this send me back to 'I can do all things through Christ who strengthens me.'"

———

Trish thought about her mother's words later that

day when her arm got bumped in the crush of students hurrying to class.

In government class, the teacher announced that all of them would be involved in class projects. "We'll divide into groups of three or four, and each team will come up with its own idea and plan. The goal is to understand more about how our democratic system functions."

Trish and Rhonda looked at each other across the aisle. How could they get on the same team?

"Now we could number off, but since we're learning about the democratic process, I will entertain ideas from the floor."

Trish and Rhonda stared at each other, raised eyebrows matching. The classroom had never been so silent.

"You mean about how we should choose teams?" The hesitant question came from the other side of the room.

"That's correct."

"Each of us choose two partners," someone then responded.

"What if someone is left out?" Ms. Wainwright shot back.

"Take the first three in a row . . ." Groans from around the room.

"Go alphabetically." More groans.

"Vote." A hush waited for the teacher's response.

"Now how would you work that out?" Added groans. The suggester shrugged.

"We could elect a committee to divide the class into groups."

Ms. Wainwright wrote their suggestions on the board as they came up. "Remember how we talked about democracy being a slow process?" She read each suggestion again. "All of these take time."

"You could assign the groups."

"True. That form of government is called a . . ." She waited for responses.

"Dictatorship."

"Monarchy." Trish glared at someone behind her who hissed at her answer.

"True, if I were the queen," Ms. Wainright said with a smile. "We're going to vote on which method to use, so raise your hands for the one you like best. Just remember, when we're finished, everyone must be on a team."

The class selected personal choice so Rhonda, Trish, and Doug formed a group. "We gotta make sure everyone's on a team." Trish checked over her shoulder to see if anyone appeared left out.

"Is everyone finished?" the teacher asked. At their nods, she shook her head. "Did you include those who are absent?"

"Who's not here?"

"We only have two," someone else said. "They can be on our team."

"Good. Now, what have you learned from this?"

"Democracy can be a pain in the . . ." one of the guys muttered.

The teacher laughed along with the class. "True. Any kind of government can. What else?"

"It takes time and cooperation," Rhonda answered.

"Good." After waiting for more answers, Ms. Wainwright finished. "Government is a method of solving problems, hopefully for the good of the greatest number of people."

"Yeah, and if you're absent, you don't have no say."

Again, the chuckles rippled around the room. "So true. So voting is a must." She started two sheets of paper down the outside aisles. "Now sign up together when the paper comes to you. Then you have five minutes to talk about your project." She raised her hand for silence. "Deadline for the topic is Friday."

"Don't we get to vote on that?"

She shook her head, laughing along with the rest.

"She's cool," Rhonda said as they left the classroom at the bell.

"Yeah, but what are we gonna do?" Doug walked beside Trish.

"Got me. Guess we could attend a trial or something." The three looked at each other and shrugged.

"How about stringing up a certain pain-in-the-neck lawyer?" Trish tossed her books in her locker. She grinned at the rolled-eye looks from her friends. "Just a thought."

When she got home from school, there was a message from Curt to call him back.

"Hi, this is Trish Evanston." She polished the apple she'd retrieved from the refrigerator.

"Guess what? Your suspicions were right on. Smithson, the assistant manager, has put two rather large deposits into his savings account in the last six months. And one in his checking. These are besides his regular paychecks."

"How'd you . . ."

"Don't ask. Let's just say I owe a computer friend of mine a favor."

"The deposits could be legal."

"Sure. But at least if we need them, the police will have some place to start."

"Whoa, this gets scary." Trish turned and, leaning her elbows on the counter, stared out the window. "Now what?"

"You suppose you could ask some questions over at the track? Just if anyone's noticed anything unusual. They'll talk with you since they all know you. Better not to have a stranger like me butting in."

"I guess." Trish munched her apple after she hung up the phone. As he'd said, at least they had a place to start. And all she'd be doing is talking with her friends at the track. Surely her mother couldn't yell at her for that.

———

Trish wasn't exactly thrilled about the topic idea her team turned in on Friday, but they hadn't thought up anything better. They would contact their local legislator and ask how they could help with her campaign. They'd probably end up stuffing envelopes.

But Saturday morning she headed to Portland Meadows. When her mother had asked why, Trish just said she'd like to see how things were going there.

That wasn't a lie. That's what she told Nagger when he started grousing.

Since many of the local trainers used the barns and track on a regular basis (not everyone had their own track like Runnin' On Farm), Trish felt right at home in the bustle. She answered all the greetings and stopped to visit with some on her way to the Diego stalls.

"Trish." Bob Diego leaped to his feet when she

thumped on the desk where he sat going over training charts. "Good to see you. You bringing your horses in?"

"No, just came to . . ."

"I know, you need some extra money, so you'll ride for me in the mornings."

Trish shook her head and laughed.

"Okay, then how about I buy you a cup of coffee?" Bob closed the book on his desk and slipped it into the drawer. "Or breakfast." He checked his watch. "Mine's long overdue."

They discussed the goings-on at the track on their way to the kitchen, and after getting their food, Trish brought up the council meeting. In an undertone, she told Diego of the money in the assistant manager's account.

"How'd you find that out?" Diego asked after chewing a mouthful of pancakes.

"Don't ask, as the man told me."

The trainer shook his head. "You better stay out of this, young lady, or your mother'll—"

"I know. I'm being careful. Just told him I'd ask around. See what the scuttlebutt is here."

After they finished eating, Diego pushed back his chair. "I better get back. Some of us have to work for a living."

Trish grinned up at him. "You could ride in the Triple Crown too."

"Cheeky kid." Diego knuckled her cheek. "You be careful."

Trish caught the gaze of a couple of jockeys at another table. Beyond them sat a table of owners/breeders. Trish noticed a new man talking with the owners she'd ridden for. Who was he, she wondered.

"Hey, come on over." Genie Stokes waved. "Haven't seen you in a coon's age."

Trish visited with them for a while, and soon others came by. But no one had heard anything for sure. Just made jokes about the new Corvette and grumbled about the possibility of the track not opening. Some thought they'd head for California maybe, others mentioned the South. None of them had met the new man.

Trish felt the weight of everybody's depression by the time she left the track. *Someone* had to do *something*; that was clear.

When she got home, she heard her mother blowing her nose in the kitchen. Marge hastily wiped away telltale tears as Trish walked into the room.

"What's wrong?" Trish felt that much-too-familiar clutch in her heart region.

"Nothing." Marge drew another tissue from her pocket and blew her nose again. "Just all of a sudden this house seemed so empty I wanted to scream." She tried to blink back the tears, but one escaped and rolled down her cheek. "Some days I miss your dad so much I . . ." She shook her head and squeezed her lips together. "I don't know . . . it'll go away again." With shaking fingers, she scrubbed at the tears that continued to fall.

Trish put her arms around her mother's waist and held on. She understood . . . oh, how she understood! They remained in each other's arms for a while before Trish leaned back.

"How about we bake some cookies for David?" Trish suggested. "I'll call Rhonda and Brad. Maybe they'd like to help. The house won't be so empty if we have a party."

Marge nodded and mopped her face again. "Let me get myself together first."

"They can." Trish hung up the phone and turned with a grin. "Said they'd be here in half an hour."

"You're pretty special, you know that, Tee?" Marge brushed back a lock of hair that refused to stay confined in Trish's braid.

"Thanks."

By the time they finished, the box for David contained chocolate chip, peanut butter, and oatmeal cookies, plus brownies. All the cookie jars bulged, and more containers made it to the freezer.

After helping Patrick, Brad went out for pizza, and the party continued, including the trainer.

When Trish fell into bed that night, she hugged herself and couldn't quit smiling. What fun they'd had. Like old times, even without David and their father. Her thank-you's to God were the music she slipped into sleep by.

————

She was totally unprepared for what happened in church the next morning. Pastor Mort read her letter, deeding the third red convertible to the congregation.

"The church council has voted to use the money from the sale of the car to begin a fund for a fifteen-passenger van to be used by all the organizations here at church." He smiled at Trish. "But especially for the youth groups."

Someone stood in the back of the church. "Why don't we change the idea from a van to a full-sized bus? Seems that would be much more practical."

"I'll pledge $1,000." Trish had no idea who volunteered that amount, but within five minutes, thousands more had been pledged. She gripped her mother's hand.

"Guess that makes it all legal, then." Pastor Mort winked at Trish. "The council will appoint a committee to find us a bus."

Pastor Ron, the youth pastor, rose to his feet. "I think we should name our bus *Hal*, in memory of Hal Evanston and in thanks to his daughter, Trish."

That did it. Trish fought down the urge to flee and instead let the tears flow. After all, if even a pastor can cry from the steps of the altar, why should the congregation do less? And from the sniffs she heard, there weren't many dry eyes in the entire place.

Marge tugged on her hand so that together they got to their feet and turned to face their church family. "Thank you." What other words were necessary?

Amidst all the community hugs and happy discussion, Trish felt like pulling a "Rhonda" and spinning in place as her friend still sometimes did when the excitement grew too great.

"You didn't tell me," Rhonda whispered when they had a moment.

"Didn't think it would be a big deal," Trish whispered back.

"Right! With Pastor Mort in on it, anything can be a big deal."

Trish returned a watery grin. "But who knew all the others would jump in like that?"

"God?"

The glow stayed with her, through the night and all day at school.

When she walked in the door at home, her mother handed her an envelope. Trish's name and address were typed on it. There was no return address.

Trish looked at her mother, shrugged, and slit open the envelope. The message leaped out at her. Letters cut from newspapers and magazines spelled out "Keep your nose out of other people's business. Stay away from Portland Meadows!"

CHAPTER TEN

She felt like she'd been slugged in the gut.

"Trish, what is it? You're white as a sheet." Trish handed her mother the piece of paper. "Oh, my . . ." Marge stared at her daughter and then read the letter again. "That's it! You are *not* to talk to anyone again. Who did you talk to? What'd you do?" Her voice rose with each word.

"Mom, Mom. I didn't do anything. I didn't say anything to anyone."

"Then why this letter?" She flicked the paper with the backs of her fingers.

"I don't know." Trish swallowed the thought of *all I did was ask a few questions, get people talking to me. Someone sure told the wrong party.* Her mind cataloged all the people she'd talked to at the track. Which one of them was the snitch?

The phone rang. Trish answered it and only muttered answers before hanging up.

"Curt is calling the cops. He got one just like this."

"Oh, wonderful! They'll be shooting at you next." Marge rubbed her forehead with her fingertips.

"This isn't television, for Pete's sake. No one's gonna hurt anyone."

124

"Famous last words."

"Mom, you're worrying again."

"With just cause."

"I gotta get down to work the horses." Trish laid the letter on the counter. "Don't worry, Mom. It'll be okay."

But Trish wasn't so sure of that when the white Portland Police cruiser pulled up to the front gate. She dismounted from her last mount of the afternoon and strode quickly up the rise. Marge was already inviting the two officers inside by the time Trish made it to the house.

"Tricia Evanston?" The man's broad shoulders made his six-foot frame seem even taller. He would have no trouble commanding respect anywhere, as far as Trish could figure, and his deep voice only added to the illusion of power. He dwarfed the woman beside him. He extended a hand that could have doubled for a baseball mitt, but when he shook Trish's hand, gentleness passed through the contact.

When Trish nodded, he continued. "I'm Officer Don Parks, and this is my partner, Sheila Dunning. We've been assigned to look into this case after Curt Donovan called the station."

"You've already talked with Curt?" Trish kept her voice from squeaking by sheer act of will. Why did meeting these officers make her want to hide under the bed? She hadn't done anything wrong.

"Yes, and we have his letter to run through some tests. Do you mind if we sit down?" He indicated the living room.

"Oh, I'm sorry," Marge said. "What happened to my manners? Can I get you a cup of coffee? Cookies?"

Trish could tell her mother had an attack of nerves

also. And she *really* hadn't done anything wrong.

"Now, may we see your letter?" Officer Dunning spoke in a musical voice. Her smile set Trish as much at ease as Parks' power made her shake.

Trish held out the letter. "It came in the mail today. Here's the envelope too." She watched as the man took the letter by the upper corner and held it out so both officers could study it at the same time.

"Looks like a match." Parks pinned Trish with laser-blue eyes. "You have an idea who would send something like this?"

Trish shook her head. "Nor why, either."

"Why don't you tell me what you know about the events at Portland Meadows, including the city council meeting."

Trish did as asked. While she talked, her mother brought in a tray with coffee mugs and cookies. The officers listened intently, writing on small notebooks but not asking questions until she finished.

Trish really felt she was finished by the time they stood up an hour later and thanked her and her mother for their time. As they left, the man turned to her.

"Watching you win the Triple Crown was some experience. You look so small and vulnerable up on that black colt of yours. My daughter talks nonstop of racing thoroughbreds someday ever since she saw you."

"Your daughter will be over six feet tall by the time she's twelve." Sheila winked at Trish. "Becky, his daughter, is a doll, but she's been the tallest in her class since kindergarten."

"Yeah, well, anyway, congratulations. You did a fine job."

"Thank you. Bring Becky by at the track sometime—

that is, if we ever get to race there."

"I will, and if you think of anything else, here's my card. Call me."

"Okay. Will you let me know if you find anything in the letter?" Trish couldn't believe she asked the question. It's just that her curiosity got ahold of her. She saw the frown that creased her mother's forehead.

"We'll see." The two left. Trish watched them walk back to their patrol car, then she turned again to her mother.

"I know, I'll stay out of it. I will." But she couldn't get the words "I promise" past the idea stage. Surely this was all over now.

The next day in government class, Ms. Wainwright opened a discussion about ways the people can influence government. They talked about voting and how important it was for eighteen-year-olds to voice their opinion too.

"How else?" The teacher nodded to a hand raised in back.

"You can attend meetings in your community and say what you think, like at the school board."

"Good. I see several teams have decided to use that for their project." She glanced down the list in a file folder.

Trish raised her hand. When the teacher acknowledged her, she began. "We have a problem at the racetrack, and it involves the Portland city council." Trish continued on with the story, bringing the class up-to-date, including the visit from the police officers.

"So, what'd they find on the letter?" one of the students asked.

Trish shrugged. "I don't know. But I feel so—so helpless. You know—who listens to kids anyway?"

"Someone must have for you to get a warning like that." Ms. Wainwright turned and began writing on the chalkboard. "Okay, class, this is what I want you to do. Turn to page 126 of your textbook. This section talks about petitions and referendums. When you are finished reading, raise your hand."

The silence after everyone found the place deepened. Trish did as she was instructed, at the same time wondering what this had to do with her problem at Portland Meadows. As she read, she grew more excited.

"That's it!" Rhonda fairly jumped in her seat. "We could get up petitions to keep the city from closing down The Meadows." She poked Trish in the side.

Trish nodded without looking up and waved Rhonda's hand away. Could she and Rhonda and Doug take *this* on as a project instead?

As soon as all hands were raised, the teacher moved back to the front of her desk and leaned against it.

"Are there any questions?"

"Could kids do this? Do you have to live in Portland? How long do we have? What do we do first?" The questions ricocheted from the walls.

"What do you think?" The teacher returned to the chalkboard. "Okay, let's lay out a plan. Step one."

"Get more information about petitions." Doug winked at Trish.

"How?"

Some volunteered to do research in the school library; someone else's team said they'd hit the Fort Vancouver Public Library; Doug said Rhonda, Trish, and he would go to City Hall in Portland and ask there.

"We will?" Rhonda shot him a questioning glance.

"Good! Day after tomorrow we'll all bring in what we've found." The buzzer rang before the teacher could finish her instructions. No one moved. "And then we'll set up a real plan of action. Let's just call this the Prairie Political Action Committee . . . PAC in political jargon. Class dismissed."

"How can you go to Portland?" Rhonda asked as the three of them left the classroom. "You've got football practice."

Doug smacked his palm against his forehead. "I got so excited in there I forgot. Guess that means you two have to go. Think you can handle it?"

"My mother's going to kill me."

"No she won't. Tell her this is a class assignment. If she's not happy about it, she can call and talk to Ms. Wainwright." Doug raised his eyebrows and shrugged. "That's all you have to do."

"You know, for a dumb jock, you make an awful lot of sense." Trish looked up at the guy walking beside her.

"Look who's calling who a dumb jock. At least my opponents don't try to mash me against steel bars or . . ."

"I get the picture." Trish held up a hand. "How about if I call Curt and have him get us all the information he can from the newspaper? The city offices probably close by five, so we better hustle. No hanging out with what's-his-name after school today, Rhonda, okay? See you guys." Trish grabbed her gym bag and headed for weight training. That should get her mind off "The Mess," as she was beginning to refer to it.

———

All the way to Portland the two girls discussed the situation and the petitions. And they always came back to "why?" Why would anyone cause problems there?

"My dad says it probably has something to do with drugs." Rhonda sipped her Diet Coke.

"Your dad thinks everything has to do with drugs." Trish braked for the car that slowed in front of them. I–5 was already slowing with pre-rush-hour traffic.

"I know, but he also said that's a prime piece of real estate, and with all the development going up around there—"

"Yeah, Patrick mentioned that too. But why would a developer send a stupid letter like I got?"

"Beats me. Jason said he wanted to help with the petitions too."

"He just wants to be wherever you are."

"No, really. Said he'd learn more about the American political system this way."

"Gimme a break."

By the time they left the courthouse, they carried bags of stuff. A booklet about drafting a petition seemed the most valuable. The people they'd talked with appeared really pleased that a group of kids was taking an interest in local government.

"Just make sure you follow all the guidelines, honey," one woman reminded them. "If it's not done exactly right, all your efforts will be wasted."

A man had volunteered to come talk to their class about running for public office. Everyone wished them well.

"They were all so helpful," Rhonda said for the third time when they got back in the car.

"Yes, Rhonda. And now, do we ever have plenty of homework to do! And I have horses to work. You want to help?"

"Sure. I don't have any shows for another month or so. George can go one day without working." Her thoroughbred Arab gelding's name was really Akbar Sadat, but they'd called him George ever since Rhonda had bought him four years earlier as a two-year-old.

Curt Donovan's tiny white car was parked by the front gate when they turned into Runnin' On Farm. They found him inside, munching cookies and visiting with Marge.

"I have a packet of stuff for you," he said after greeting them both. "I hit the paper archives. Amazing the stuff you can find down there."

"Yeah, and look what we got at the courthouse." Trish dumped their armloads on the table. "And I have horses to work, so let me change and I'll be right back." She didn't look at her mother. She could feel the frown all the way down the hall.

Curt strolled down to the barns with them. "I seem to be hitting a dead end with my investigations. Without a court order, I can't find out where Smithson got his money. When I tried to talk with him, he hung up, and ever since then he's been out whenever I call or go by."

"Maybe he left the country," Rhonda said.

"No, his Corvette is parked in its usual place. What a fool if that money was a bribe!"

"What are the police doing?"

"Nothing that I can tell. Letters like that are pretty small stuff compared to all the cases they try to solve." Trish and Rhonda groaned in unison.

"Yeah, somebody has to get killed before the cops take any action." Rhonda was being her dramatic self.

"They did come talk to me—and they seemed to care."

"Caring isn't the problem. Lack of time, money, and personnel are the issues. Thanks to city budget cuts, the police department has been taking it in the neck." Curt greeted Patrick and Brad, who already had three horses saddled.

"We'll be about an hour." Trish raised her knee for a leg up.

"I better get going. See you." Curt turned and strode back up the rise to his car.

"I think he likes you."

"Rhonda!"

Brad just shook his head as they trotted the horses out to the track. "Patrick wanted to work the gates today."

"I know, but we had to do our school assignment first." Rhonda could sound real self-righteous when she tried.

————

Later that evening Trish had just finished her zoology assignment when her mother knocked on her bedroom door. "Can I come in?"

"Sure." Trish stretched her arms above her head and yawned. "You don't happen to have a Diet Coke with you, do you?"

Marge shook her head. "I'll be right back." She returned in a couple of minutes, a glass filled with ice and Diet Coke in her hand. "Here you go."

"Thanks. That was really nice of you." Trish sipped and rotated her shoulders. She waited for what she knew was coming.

Marge sat down on the bed. "I asked you not to get involved with the investigation."

"I know and I'm not."

"Then what about all this?" Marge waved a hand over the papers stacked on Trish's bed.

"That's an assignment for my government class. We're studying local government and how ordinary people can influence those in office." Trish parroted her teacher's words. "You can check with Ms. Wainwright if you like."

"And the situation at The Meadows has nothing to do with this?"

What could Trish say? She gathered her thoughts before answering. The truth was always best, her father always said.

"I brought up The Meadows because she was talking about ordinary people influencing government, like I said. I just thought we'd kick it around a bit, but she got all excited and pretty soon everyone was volunteering to do the research, and Doug said our team would pick up stuff at the courthouse, and so here I am."

Marge nodded, one fingertip on her chin. "You know, Tee, I just don't want you to get hurt."

"How could I get hurt? I'm just studying government." She didn't say, "You worry too much," even though she wanted to. Sometimes keeping your mouth shut was smarter than spouting off.

By the time Trish read all the stuff they'd collected, she felt like her head was stuffed. You didn't just walk in and come out ten minutes later with a petition in hand and start collecting signatures. She glanced at the clock. Five to midnight. And she hadn't yet written the paper due in English. Here school hadn't been going two weeks and she was already behind.

She drew her notebook out and started writing. Two

pages taking the pro side of an issue. "Should Horse Racing Continue at Portland Meadows?" Easy topic. She sure knew plenty about it.

She closed her books at twelve-thirty and climbed into bed. At least she didn't have to be up at four to work horses at the track before school. That would have gone on the . . . She fell asleep before she could finish the thought.

———————

Her class spent the next three days working on their petition. On Monday they car-pooled over to the courthouse and submitted their final forms. The clerk looked them over, read their application, assigned it a number, and typed in the required information. When they left they had the original ready to make copies.

Curt and another reporter, along with a photographer, met them on the courthouse steps. After asking questions, they lined the class up and, with Ms. Wainwright standing to the side, took pictures.

"Now, where are you going to collect signatures?" Curt asked.

"At a couple of malls and several grocery stores. We have to make copies first, so that won't start until tomorrow."

"Some of us are going to go house to house," one of the boys said. "We're working in teams of three so we'll be plenty safe."

"Since it's Saturday, we can work all day," Rhonda added.

All the student teams had their assignments, along with clipboards, extra copies of the petition, and plenty of pens, by the time they left school late that afternoon.

Trish, Doug, and Rhonda had volunteered to work at Clackamas Town Center to the southeast of Portland. "That way we can go shopping afterwards," Rhonda whispered. Trish just shook her head. Shopping and guys had gone to her friend's head.

They had their spiels down pat the next morning when the four of them—Jason came along like he promised—arrived at the huge mall.

"Now remember, qualify them first. Ask if they are registered voters 'cause otherwise their signature won't count." Trish opened her trunk to remove their box of supplies.

By the end of their two-hour stint, Trish felt as if her tongue would stick to the roof of her mouth, it was so dry. Her shoulders ached, her feet hurt, and her friends suffered the same.

"I'm starved." Rhonda sank down on a bench overlooking the central courtyard. "Let's head for the food."

"We have to wait for Jennifer and her team. They'll be here any minute. Just keep at this 'til they come." Trish pushed herself to her feet. "Come on, not much longer." She walked over to a woman coming in the door. "Please, ma'am, we have a petition here to keep Portland Meadows Race Track open. Are you a registered voter?" When the woman nodded, Trish extended the clipboard. "Would you be willing to sign here?"

Trish saw the other team push open the doors. Help had arrived.

———

The story and pictures hit the front page of *The Oregonian*'s Sunday edition. The class stood grinning on the courthouse steps, and the article said, "More pictures and story inside." There was a close-up of Rhonda with her clipboard and someone signing it. Trish was quoted several times. An accompanying article by Curt Donovan detailed the situation at The Meadows.

"At least my picture isn't in it." Trish broke the uncomfortable silence as she and her mother drove to church.

"Oh, no? Second from the right, first row. You and all your classmates." Marge clenched her hands on the steering wheel. "Couldn't you at least have stood behind somebody?"

At school the next day, the fourth-period American Government class rated hero status. Copies of the articles wore out from being passed hand to hand.

"Cool. Awesome. Good picture. Bad picture." The raves depended on who was speaking.

"I'm really proud of all of you," their teacher said. "So far we have collected 5,000 signatures. And we have a week to go."

Different kids shared their experiences as signature gatherers. Most of the comments from the people they'd talked to had been favorable.

Trish came out of weight-training class feeling high both physically and mentally. What a day this had been!

She waved goodbye to Doug on his way to football practice and crossed the parking lot to her car. A crowd of students surrounded it.

They parted like the Red Sea, all voices silent as Trish approached.

Big block letters scratched in the sides of her car read, "Stay out of PM or ELSE!"

Trish thought she would throw up.

Chapter Eleven

"Go tell Mr. Adams."

Trish heard the voice as if from a long tube. Her car, her beautiful car. She knelt beside the door and traced the hateful words with a shaking finger. Why would anyone do such a thing?

"Trish." Rhonda knelt beside her. "Maybe you shouldn't touch it—there might be evidence, you know."

Trish snatched her hand back. "What have I done to make someone do this?" She could feel the tears running down her face but did nothing to stop them.

"Okay, let's move back. Come on, kids. Let me through." Mr. Adams' voice preceded his arrival.

Trish rose to her feet, feeling as if she were pushing the entire county up with her. She read the words again and walked around the car, seeing the entire damage for the first time. The same words were scrawled on the passenger side and a tic-tac-toe game covered the trunk.

"Are you all right, Trish?" the principal asked when he joined her.

Trish shook her head. "Umm, my car." She wiped her cheeks with her fingertips.

"But you weren't hurt?"

"It was like that when we got here. We saw it first.

137

Trish didn't get here 'til a minute ago." One of the guys who answered was parked right next to the red convertible.

"I had Mrs. Olson call the police. They'll be here soon." Mr. Adams raised his voice from talking with Trish. "The rest of you go on home now, unless any of you saw strangers in the parking lot."

The crowd broke up. Trish could hear their conversations, but she didn't respond. She clamped her arms across her chest to still the shaking. Inside, the old rage sputtered and sparked.

The police cut their siren when they reached the drive to Prairie High School. Their flashing light-bar helped clear the way for them to park next to Trish's damaged car.

The two male officers introduced themselves before one began questioning those still around, while the other studied the damage. But no one had seen anything. No one had heard anything unusual.

"Do you patrol the parking lot?" one officer asked Mr. Adams.

"Not really, but there are always people coming and going. Surely someone would have seen strangers out here."

"Could this be the prank of a student? Anyone have any grudges?" He asked this last question of Trish, who shook her head.

"It's like that letter she got," Rhonda said. "Tell them, Trish."

After she told her story, she looked up to see the officer studying her. "You sure have ticked someone off. Any idea who?"

"The only one I know might be involved is Smithson,

the assistant manager at the track. The Portland police are investigating him for problems at Portland Meadows."

"Do you know who's in charge of that investigation?"

Trish dug in her purse for the officer's business card and gave it to the sheriff depute. He copied the information into his notebook and handed back the card.

"If there's no more, can I go home now?"

"Do you have a ride?" The officer snapped his notebook shut and stuck it back in the khaki shirt pocket.

"My car . . ."

"We'll need to tow it in and go over it for fingerprints. Though I'm not sure what good it will do, not if all those kids touched it."

"When can I have it back?"

"Depends."

"I'll go call my mom." Rhonda turned and headed back inside.

Trish swallowed hard to trap the screams she felt in her throat. She sucked in a deep breath and looked across the parking lot to the fir trees on the other side of the road. "Depends on what?"

"Look, miss, if this car is involved in a felony of any kind, we have to impound it for evidence. From what you say, a felony may have been committed at the track. And it's under investigation, so we would be remiss in not impounding evidence."

The guy talked like he'd just memorized the textbook. Trish recrossed her arms over her chest and gritted her teeth.

They were going to take her car.

"Look, it's still locked." She pointed in the window. "And they didn't touch anything in there. Can I please open the door and get my stuff out?" If she spoke precisely enough, maybe she could keep the tears at bay. Why, oh why, did she have to cry when she was so furious she could have chewed the man up and spit him out?

"Give me your keys and I'll open it for you. Then just touch your jacket and bag. They may have forced the lock, put something inside, and locked it up again."

Trish looked to the side and down to the ground. If he didn't start talking like a human being she might flip out.

"Easy, Trish, he's just doing his job." Mr. Adams laid a firm hand on her shoulder.

Trish wasn't sure if it was to help her control herself or to offer comfort. But whichever, it helped. She took in another deep breath and handed the deputy the keys.

"My mom's coming right away," Rhonda panted after dashing across the parking lot.

Trish could feel the anger bubbling and snorting down in her midsection. All the way home, she answered questions in monosyllables while she tried to figure it out. Why her? Why her car?

"Well, at least it's better damaging the car than you, Trish," Mrs. Seaboldt said, her voice calming and so very reasonable.

"Yeah." Trish agreed in voice, but her insides would have no part of it. *Of course it is. But why damage anything? What's going on over there that's so important— maybe someone is running drugs like Rhonda said.*

Marge was working on the farm books at the rolltop desk in the living room when Trish slammed in the door. "What happened, Tee? You're so late." She finished her entry before raising her head.

At the look on her daughter's face, she shoved the

rolling chair back and leaped to her feet, catching Trish in her arms.

The fury let loose in tears.

Marge looked across her sobbing daughter's head to meet the matching blue eyes of Rhonda and Dot Seaboldt. "Trish's car was keyed. The police are impounding it." Rhonda patted Trish's heaving shoulder.

"Keyed?"

"Someone scratched it up."

"Actually, the message was . . ."

"The message?" Marge interrupted. "What in the world is going on here?"

"It said "Stay out of PM or ELSE!" on both sides and a tic-tac-toe game scrawled on the trunk."

"Oh, my . . . ! Are you all right?" Marge stepped back to study her daughter.

"Yes! Mother, it's my c-a-r!"

"Cars can be replaced. Daughters can't." Marge clutched Trish to her chest but let her go when Trish jerked back.

"How can you be so calm? I—my car—" Trish sucked in a breath that finally made it past the boulders blocking her throat. "They won't give me my car back for months."

"So, you can drive the van. I'll use the pickup." Marge handed her daughter a tissue. Her clipped words said she wasn't as calm as she acted.

"You want me to come back and help with the horses?" Rhonda asked.

"I guess. With my luck, I'll probably get dumped and break a leg."

"Trish!" Marge's order cut through Trish's self-pity. "We'll hear no talk like that!"

Trish started to say something but clamped her mouth shut instead.

"Now, where is that card Officer Parks gave you?"

"In my purse, why?"

"To let them know what happened. It's time for someone to get serious about this—now!"

Trish dug in her purse and handed her mother the business card.

"I take it we're not going out to collect petition signatures tonight?" Rhonda asked.

"No, you're not, at least Trish isn't." Marge's tone brooked no argument. When Trish started to sputter, one look did her in.

"But *I* am."

"Me too." Dot added her vote. "And tomorrow during the day, I'm available too."

"There's a TBA meeting tonight." Trish hesitated to remind her mother.

"Fine. You go take care of the horses—I've already worked with the babies—and I'll meet you there. I'll pick you up, Dot, in say . . ." Marge checked her watch, "half an hour."

"I'll be ready in fifteen minutes." Dot took her daughter by the arm. "I'll bring Rhonda back with me."

Trish and Rhonda looked at each other, their total shock evident in wide eyes and shut mouths.

"Oh, and call Curt. Ask him for the DA's number. Tell him about the meeting and that I want a few minutes to talk with him." Trish did as she was told.

————————

Later that evening after the meeting, Trish wanted to rehash the events with her mother, but Marge said she had letters to write. Trish worked on her zoology and then ambled into the kitchen for a drink and an apple. Just then the phone rang.

"David!" Trish's squeal brought Marge on the line too. After they exchanged greetings David said, "Thanks for the goodies. I still have some hidden in a box under my bed."

"Under your bed, yuk. Along with all the dirty socks and . . ."

"Listen, bird brain, I'll have you know we vacuumed just last—uh, last week."

"Okay, children," Marge interrupted their banter, "knock it off. Tell him what's gone on here, Tee, and I'll add what you miss."

"Maybe I better come home," David said when they'd brought him up-to-date.

"What good would that do?" Marge asked. "We'll handle it. You are going to Kentucky, though, aren't you?"

"I guess. I haven't really given it a lot of thought. How many horses are you taking?"

"Only Firefly." Trish hugged the phone to her ear. This was the first time her mother talked about Kentucky like it was a for-sure thing. Even though they'd paid the earlier racing fees, they still could back out. "Adam's taking two others, running one in the Breeder's Cup."

"He gonna have Red ride for him?" David's chuckle echoed over the line. "How is he anyway?"

"Fine, last I heard."

"I can't believe they keyed your car." David returned to the earlier discussion.

"Me either. Take care of yourself, brother. You're the only one I've got."

"I'm not the one in trouble. You ever thought of keeping your mouth shut?" He groaned. "Don't answer that. Love you guys."

Trish took her treats and returned to her bedroom, resolved to read a chapter in English and write to Red. By the time she finished the letter, her eyes refused to focus. She signed it "Thinking of you" and "Yours, Trish." She thought about signing "Love, Trish," but she couldn't.

Did she love him? What did love really mean? Sure she felt all warm and melty inside when he held her hand. And yes, the kisses were nice. No, nice was far too . . . too . . . nice a word. She *liked* kissing Red and being kissed back. But was this love? More than love between two friends? *Real* love?

She clicked off the desk lamp and got ready for bed. After crawling under the covers, she took her Bible from the bedside table and flipped it open to her verse for the night. She chuckled when she read the first part. "Count it all joy, my brethren, when you meet various trials . . ." Guess you could call what she'd been going through "trials."

But the "count it all joy" . . . now that was the sticky part.

You haven't even been giving God the glory like you promised, Nagger whispered in her ear. *Let alone counting it joy. What happened to giving thanks for all things?*

Trish nodded. He was right. She finished reading the verse. ". . . for you know that the testing of your faith produces steadfastness. And let steadfastness have its full effect, that you might be perfect and complete, lacking in nothing."

Now, perfect and complete, that sounded pretty good. She closed the book and put it away. "God, how am I supposed to do all this? And you know, it doesn't really make a lot of sense."

She waited, as if hoping for a mighty voice to explain all these goings-on. Outside, the branches of the tree scraped against the house in the night breeze. Beside her bed, the clock ticked as the number panels fell to the next minute.

"What am I supposed to do? What's going to happen?" She sighed. What a mystery. She clutched the blanket under her chin. What was happening was she was changing from girl-super-jockey to girl-sleuth, and she'd never read a mystery in her life.

She lay in the quiet. *So I just give thanks and count it all joy—right?* Her song trickled through her mind. She hummed along with it. How easy to picture eagle's wings and soaring over the earth. She snuggled deeper. And those large, warm hands holding her. She fell asleep with a smile on her face and a matching one in her heart.

––––––––––

"Curt's story hit the front page." Marge handed the paper across the table. "He writes well."

Trish studied the story of the TBA meeting and the continuing investigation. "At least he didn't quote me this time," she said after finishing the bottom few paragraphs about the students gathering petition signatures. "Mom?"

"Ummm?"

"You remember that new man at the meeting last night?"

"Sure, why?" Marge lowered her paper.

"He looks so familiar, like I've seen him before, but I can't remember when." Trish rubbed her forehead with the fingertips of both hands.

"His name was—ah—Highstreet, Kendal Highstreet. He's a businessman up from California, thinking of buying a farm up here since land prices are so outrageous in California. He wants to breed and race thoroughbreds."

"That's it. I saw him at the track kitchen the morning I went over there. He was sitting with . . ." Trish scrunched her eyes closed, trying to see the picture again. ". . . With a couple of owners and Ward Turner, the track manager."

"So?"

Trish shrugged. "I don't know. Just seemed important somehow." She carefully brushed toast crumbs into her palm and dusted them off over the plate. "You doing anything special today?"

"I'll let you know more when I do." Marge disappeared behind her paper again.

Trish drained the last of her milk and got to her feet. Her mother's curious response bugged her all the way to Rhonda's.

"You thought anything about your birthday yet?" Rhonda asked. "It's only two days away."

"I'm not having a birthday this year."

"Trish, why that's the stupidest thing I ever heard."

Trish rolled her eyes and sniffed. Good thing they were stopped at a stop sign. How could her mood change so fast? Raindrops splattered on the windshield.

How fitting. Tears both outside and in. And here she'd promised herself no more crying. Especially after the storms of yesterday.

————

"You need to pay better attention, lass," Patrick reminded her when she brought the bay gelding back to the stables that afternoon. "He nearly dumped you out there."

"I know." Trish patted the deep red neck and jumped to the ground. Sure she knew enough to pay attention. And her inattention nearly cost her. Blowing leaves were enough to spook any horse, but a good rider would have anticipated his reaction—been prepared.

She was reminded again when they worked each of the horses through the starting gates. Old gray Dan'l acted as instructor and tranquilizer, pacing through the gate without the flicker of an ear. But one of the fillies didn't care for the tight squeeze and bolted—or rather tried to. Trish caught her in time.

"Tomorrow we'll close the front gate and let them stand there." Patrick slipped the saddle off the filly. "You two wash this one down and I'll take care of Dan'l. Oh, Brad, Marge said to remind you about supper tonight."

"You mean dinner?" Brad winked at Trish. Patrick still couldn't get used to calling the evening meal dinner.

"Whatever. Just get busy, you two, or we'll eat without you." Patrick went back to his brushing of the gray gelding.

Trish and Brad could hear him muttering about "smart aleck kids," but they knew he was teasing. She wondered sometimes if he didn't say some things just to get a rise out of them.

They'd finished dinner before Marge brought up the reason for the family meeting. Trish scraped the plates, stacked them, and carried them in to the sink. On her return, she brought the coffeepot and poured three cups. She only felt like drinking coffee in the morning and then at the track.

"I was hoping you could go to Kentucky with us," she was saying to Brad. "With all you've done, I thought you might like a trip."

"Would I! Old David will be there too?" At Marge's nod, he said, "Good."

"Adam called today and asked if we'd decided yet when or if we were bringing the horses back up. Or if we were bringing others down. Either way, he has to arrange for stalls, so he needs to know. I told him what's happened here and that we still don't know if The Meadows will open or not."

"When does he have to know?" Patrick pulled on one earlobe, a sure sign that he was thinking.

"Soon. Also he wants to schedule races for those down there if they are going to stay."

Trish could feel the slow burn starting again. "Well, why not leave them there? I haven't raced for so long, I've probably forgotten how." She shoved her chair back and stood up. "I have homework to do. Whatever you decide is fine with me."

Liar! That seemed to be one of Nagger's favorite names for her. He repeated it as she strode down the hall.

———

The argument the next night had been raging for hours. At least it seemed so to Trish. Except *she* was the only one raging. Her mother sat calmly in her chair, knitting.

"How about if we go out to dinner, like we always have?"

"Mother, I don't want to go out to dinner. It won't be like it's always been because Dad and David aren't here."

"Choose something else then."

"That's the point. I am choosing. It's my choice and I choose to do nothing."

"We could get pizza with Brad and Rhonda—invite Patrick. I bet he hasn't had birthday cake for years. Rent a movie."

"You don't get it, do you? We're—I'm skipping my birthday this year." She started to leave the room. "The rest of you can go do whatever you want."

It was the worst birthday of her life.

CHAPTER TWELVE

"Trish, you're going to be late for school."

"No, I won't. I'm not going." Trish pulled the covers over her aching head and burrowed down into that cocoon of gray where pain didn't hurt so bad and the crack in her heart didn't show.

"Are you running a fever?" Marge sat down on the bed and felt Trish's forehead. "Sore throat?"

Trish wished she could lie. "I hurt all over but it's not a cold." A tear squeezed from under her clenched eyelid.

"The old black pit?"

Trish nodded. "Maybe if I sleep more today, I'll feel like going tomorrow."

"You know you're letting people down?"

Trish nodded.

"Yourself most of all."

Who cares? Trish wanted to scream. *Who gives a flying fig? Just get off my case!* But she didn't. Screaming was far too much trouble. Took far too much energy. When she sensed Nagger *tisking* on her shoulder, she snatched a tissue from the box and tried to blow him away. Her head hurt. Maybe she *was* coming down with a cold after all.

"Trish, I know how you feel. When your dad's and my

151

anniversary rolled around, I felt like crawling in a hole and pulling it in after me, too. The grief group helped me through a real rough time. I know the one for teens could help you."

"I'll think about it, okay?" Her tone said *just leave me alone.*

Marge remained sitting silently on the bed for a time, then stood with a sigh. "Hiding out isn't the best way to handle this, Tee. Trust me, I know."

You sure do, Trish thought. *You checked out for days.*

And what good did it do? Nagger chimed in. *You know better than this. What happened to all that joy and giving God the glory?* Sticking her fingers in her ears didn't help.

Trish tried to go back to sleep, but by now she was wide awake. Even deep breathing to relax failed to bring oblivion. Finally she threw back the covers and headed for the shower. So she missed first period. She'd make it on time for second.

"You look awful," Rhonda said when they met at the locker before lunch.

"Thanks."

"Your mom said you were hiding out."

"Yeah, well, she's a big help."

"Trish, the grief group meets this afternoon. I know things are rough for you right now, but this could help. I'll go with you."

Trish shoved her books in her locker and almost climbed in after them. With her face hidden in the locker, she gave up. "All right, I'll go." She jerked upright and glared at Rhonda. "But that doesn't mean I'll say anything." She slammed the metal door. "And then both you and my mother can get off my back!"

Rhonda didn't say anything through lunch, and the others at the table saw the scowl on Trish's face and left her alone.

When he got up to leave, Doug Ramstead laid a hand on her shoulder. "It'll get better," he whispered in her ear.

Trish pushed to her feet and fled the room.

———

The group met at the local Methodist church. Trish parked in the graveled parking lot and ordered her fingers to unclench from around the steering wheel. They were as reluctant as the rest of her. When she finally slammed the van door, Rhonda came around the vehicle, put an arm around her friend's shoulders and squeezed. Together they walked up the four stairs to the front of the cedar-sided building. A sign with an arrow pointed to a comfortably furnished room with bookshelves along one wall and a fireplace on another. Extra chairs joined the sofas and easy chairs in a circle. Half of them held teens of varying ages.

A young woman stood and extended her hand. "Hi, I'm Jessica Walden, the facilitator for this bunch. Welcome."

Trish put on her company manners and introduced both herself and Rhonda. "My mom thinks this group will help me and Rhonda—" She didn't say "dragged me here," but anyone of sensitivity could hear it.

"Came along for moral support." Rhonda beamed as if she'd just won a jumping trophy.

"You don't have to talk if you don't want to, Trish," Jessica said. "And you can call me Jessie. I even answer to 'hey you' on occasion. We'll have everyone introduce themselves when we start. If you want something to drink first, there's sodas in the fridge or ice water."

Trish declined even though her mouth felt stuffed with cotton balls. The butterflies trapped in her stomach flipped and flopped, seeking release.

When the kids started introducing themselves, Trish almost ran again. But when her turn came, she lifted her chin, gave her name, and finished with, "My father died of cancer in June."

She listened to the others share their feelings and fears, all the while fighting back her own tears. When someone started to cry, Jessie passed the tissue box, and the two on either side of the girl patted her shoulders or rubbed her back.

I'm not gonna talk. I'm not gonna talk. Trish repeated the words like a rap song. She went into a state of shock when her mouth said, "I just had a birthday and my father wasn't here for it."

"Your first holiday?" someone asked.

Trish nodded.

"That's always the worst. Christmas will be really rough too," someone else chimed in.

"This group helped me get through those first 'happy' occasions." The girl on Trish's left looked at her with caring deep in her brown eyes. "Happy they weren't. But I got through, and now the depression doesn't hit me so hard."

"You were depressed?"

The girl nodded. "We all have been, one time or another or all the time."

"Whatever fits," someone else added.

"We learn here to take it one day at a time," Jessie said. "And that there are others who've been there who can be there for us now."

"Sometimes I get so mad I—" Trish swallowed hard.

"Yep . . . yeah . . . me too . . . sure . . . right on." The voices echoed around the circle.

Trish leaned back in her chair. "So what do you do?"

"Talk it out. Run. Cry 'til it's over. Pray. Call one of my friends here." Again the answers came from around the circle.

"Just don't stuff it," Jessie said.

"Or try to tough it out." The girl next to Trish patted her arm. "Talk. Call me." She wrote her phone number on a piece of paper and handed it to Trish. "My name's Angela."

Trish left the room feeling two tons lighter than when she went in. "You don't have to go with me next week," she told Rhonda as they walked back to the van. "Thanks for coming today. And making me come."

"I didn't *make* you."

"Wanna bet?" Now she owed just about everyone in her life an apology.

The next day in government class, Ms. Wainwright made a major announcement. "We did it! You did it. You collected more than five thousand signatures over the necessary number. The county clerk figured that even with all the mistakes and people signing twice, we're well over our goal."

The class broke into cheers.

"So, Trish, the results will be presented to the city council at their next meeting. Why don't you come up and tell us what has been happening at Portland Meadows lately?"

Trish got to her feet, her butterflies suddenly doing

their flip-flop routine. When she turned to face the class she remembered why she'd rather race. *There* she didn't have to say anything.

"All the thoroughbred and quarter-horse owners and trainers are going ahead with training as if the track will open on time. The program for the season is all planned, so we've been paying pre-race fees just like we always do.

"Some of the trainers are at the track, but we still have our horses at home since we have a half-mile training track there. Four of our best horses are still down in California, where I raced this summer."

"Where's Spitfire?" someone asked.

"Back in Kentucky at BlueMist Farms, where he will stand at stud this winter. I went back to visit him over Labor Day weekend."

"What if our petitions don't work and the track never opens?" a boy asked from a seat by the windows.

Trish took a moment to answer. *That* had been the big question on her mind forever it seemed. "Some of the trainers are talking about racing in other parts of the country. Lots of the smaller stable owners will probably sell out or send their horses to trainers elsewhere. That costs a lot, so unless you have a really good horse, you wouldn't do that."

"What happened about your car?"

"Got me."

Mutual groans came from the back. Everyone knew about her bright red convertible, now impounded. When she saw no more hands, Trish started back to her seat. She paused and then said, "All of us at the track want to thank you for what you did. They were pretty impressed that you took the time to collect signatures. Thanks."

"Aw, Ms. Wainwright made us do it. No big deal."

Trish returned to her seat under cover of the laughter that broke out.

"You'll keep us posted then, Trish?" the teacher asked.

Trish just wished she had more to tell them. Who *was* responsible for the troubles at Portland Meadows? What was happening with the police investigation? How come she hadn't heard from Curt lately? She returned to reality in time to hear the assignment. "Describe your experiences collecting signatures and what you learned."

What had she learned? The whole thing wasn't over yet.

When she got home a message lay on the counter for her to call Curt. Trish dialed the Portland number and tucked the phone onto her shoulder while she flipped through the stack of mail. A card from Red. This was certainly her day. A picture of Garfield clutching his chest made her smile. The inside read, "I'm dying to hear from you." Trish giggled. At least she'd written him a letter, so they'd crossed in the mail.

Curt's voice interrupted her thoughts. "Trish, they indicted Smithson. He's in jail right now, and from what I heard, singing like a canary."

"Yes!" Trish pumped the air with a closed fist. "So now what's going to happen?"

"Hopefully, they'll snag whoever's behind all this and Portland Meadows can get on with business. I'll let you know as soon as I hear any more."

Trish hung up and danced all the way down the hall. Surely now the council would see the truth and reopen the track. She changed clothes and, after grabbing an apple, jogged down to the barns, Caesar barking and leaping beside her.

"That's wonderful," Marge said, never taking her eyes from Miss Tee working on the lunge line. The filly tossed her head and nickered when she saw Trish. Maybe all those carrots pieces were finally paying off. "Okay, girl, we'll quit for today." Marge looped the line over her arm and drew the filly in. "Good job, little one. Isn't she getting prettier all the time?"

Trish agreed. The young horse was filling out, and she carried her head with the same style Spitfire did. Even though she'd be racing a year late because of her late birth, she had all the earmarks of a winner. Trish rubbed the filly's ears and the tiny white star set smack in the middle of the broad forehead.

"I can't wait to train you," she murmured, scratching all the while. "Wait 'til you see that crowd and hear them cheering for you. You're gonna love it." The filly nibbled Trish's fingers and nosed her pocket for the treat that usually hid there. "Sorry, kid. I haven't filled my pockets yet." The two of them led the filly back to the stall and cross-tied her there for a good brushing.

"Maybe we'll be able to call Adam and tell him to ship our horses home at the same time as he leaves for Kentucky. I sure would love to ride Sarah's Pride in the Hal Evanston Handicap." Trish opened the office refrigerator and dug in the carrot sack. She used the knife on the table and cut the carrots into thick slices.

"That's a mile, you know, lass." Patrick sat down in the old-fashioned wooden office chair at the desk. "We'll have to ask Adam if she's ready for that." He tipped his stained fedora back on his head. "Or you could run Firefly, rather than shipping her to Kentucky."

"Fat chance. She's going to win with the big guys." Trish munched one of the carrot slices herself. "Hi, Brad, you hear the news?"

"Hi, all." Brad greeted them, then answered Trish. "No, what?"

Trish brought him up-to-date. "So we can start racing soon. Won't that be great?" Trish ignored the air of caution she could feel coming from both her mother and Patrick. They *were* going to start running soon. They had to.

When they got back up to the house, the message light was blinking on the answering machine. Curt's voice sounded like he was scraping bottom. "Smithson fingered Turner. Says he was behind it all, so really, things are in a worse mess than ever."

Trish felt her heart drop down around her ankles. *God, when are you going to straighten all this out?* Her groan of misery sounded more like an accusation than a prayer of praise, Nagger leaped to remind her. She could actually see the pit yawning before her when she lay down on the bed in her room, the back of her hand hiding eyes dry and gritty with unshed tears.

"I just can't believe Ward Turner would do such a thing," Trish said that night at the dinner table. "He loves horse racing with a passion."

"True." Marge spread ketchup on her hamburger and added lettuce. "But you never know what some people will do when a great deal of money is involved."

"But Curt never said there'd been money in Turner's bank account."

"Maybe he didn't look there. The Corvette is what made everyone suspicious of Smithson."

"Yeah, right." Trish nibbled on a potato chip, her mind whirling. "Smithson is out of jail now too, Curt said." She leaned back in her chair. "Think I'll go over to The Meadows tomorrow after school."

"What for?" Marge's "mother" tone took over.

"I don't know. Maybe just being there will give me some ideas. Besides, being there sometimes helps me feel closer to Dad."

"Then I'll go with you. We can both use some of your dad's wisdom right about now."

What could Trish say?

"Maybe I'll leave school early so we won't be so late working the horses here."

"Maybe not." Marge now *wore* her "mother" look, along with the sound of her voice.

Trish had a hard time with her homework that evening. Her gaze kept returning to the verses posted on the wall above her desk. One in particular seemed to stand out. "If any of you lacks wisdom, let him ask God, who gives to all men generously and without reproaching and it will be given him." Trish substituted her name for "all men," putting herself into the scripture like her father had taught her.

"If I, Trish, lack wisdom, I will ask God who gives to Trish generously and without reproaching, and the wisdom will be given to me." She cupped her chin in her hands and propped her elbows on the desk. "So, God, I'm asking for wisdom. I sure want to know what to do."

A song from Bible camp tiptoed into her mind. ". . . Give God the glory, glory. Rise and shine and give God the glory, glory . . . children of the Lord."

Trish shook her head. That didn't seem to be doing anything. She'd better get back to her homework. There was to be a quiz in zoology in the morning. She hummed along with the song while she studied the list of Latin names. How come zoology was fun and chemistry had been such a bear? She shrugged off the question. She still hated even the thought of chemistry.

The next afternoon when Trish and her mother drove into the parking lot in front of The Meadows, a bright red Corvette occupied one of the reserve parking places near the entrance. Next to it sat a silver BMW.

"Looks like Smithson is back at work," Trish commented. "You'da thought they'd have fired him."

"Maybe he's cleaning out his office." Marge turned to study the cars. "That's an out-of-state license on the gray car. Must have bucks to be driving that beauty."

They parked the minivan on the south side of the weathering grandstand and entered by the gate the golfers used. All of them were gone for the day so the nine-hole golf course laid out in the infield appeared nearly as desolate as the rest of the track in the gray of an overcast day. The triangular flags at the holes snapped in the breeze and made Trish shiver.

Off to the left and above them, the sheet of windows overlooked the track, metallic-gray like the clouds scudding above them.

Trish shivered again. "Wish I'd worn a warmer jacket."

"It is chilly. See over there to the curve. That's where you went down that day. I thought sure you were dead."

"Have you heard about the Snyder family, how they're doing?"

"I think she went back to live near her parents, someplace in the Midwest sticks in my mind. Come to think of it, we got a beautiful card from her after your father's death. She said she sure knew how we felt." Marge leaned on the fence rail. "I don't know if death coming instantly like that or prolonged like Hal's is easier."

"They're both awful." Trish turned from studying the infield and looked up at the grandstand behind them. "Seems almost spooky here. The whole thing needs re-painting, and they haven't even washed the windows yet. It's as if they don't really plan on racing here this year at all." She heard a horse whinny from the barns on the east side of the track. At least something was alive around here.

"You suppose the rest rooms are open? I need to use one." Marge turned back to the grandstand.

"Sure. We'll go up through the tunnel and use the one in the women's dressing room." Trish, hands in her windbreaker pockets, led the way up the tunnel to the circular saddling paddock. The gate from the paddock squawked in the silence, echoing in the cavernous room.

The door to the women's dressing room was locked. "We'll go to the public rooms up near the lobby. They'll be open for the office workers." She felt like tiptoeing, the smish of her tennis shoes sounding an intrusion. Why hadn't anyone turned on the lights?

When they reached the door, Marge pushed it open and disappeared inside. Trish started to follow her, but angry voices made her pause. She held the door so it shut without a sound.

Light from the huge windows in the entrance left shadows in the vaulted lobby. Trish halted her silent passage just where the hall opened into the foyer. The voice came from the offices to her left.

"But I need more money!"

A chair screeched back.

"I paid you. It's not my fault you were so stupid to buy a flashy car."

"Yeah, well I gotta get outta here. They'll figure out that Turner didn't do anything and come back to me. If you don't pony up, I'll be forced to tell'em everything I know."

Trish knew who whined. Smithson, the assistant manager. But who was the other? She forced herself to stay glued to the wall. If she moved they might see her.

"You stupid . . ." A stream of names, including a few Trish hadn't heard before, made her glad her mother wasn't there.

"All I need is a hundred thou. You won't miss it when you get this place, and it would set me up for life in Mexico. Help me out this time and I swear you'll never hear from me again."

"There's nothing that can tie you back to me."

"I'll tell them everything, I swear I will."

"Put that phone down, you imbecile." Where had Trish heard that voice?

"What are you doing with that gun?"

CHAPTER THIRTEEN

Trish darted back down the hallway.

"What's the rush?" Marge caught her as the two of them nearly collided. Trish shook her head and put a finger over her lips to signify silence. When she located the phone on the wall, her hands were shaking so badly she could hardly dial 911.

"Speak up, please," the woman on the line said clearly.

"I can't," Trish whispered as distinctly as she could. "Please, there's a man waving a gun in the lobby at Portland Meadows. I'm not sure if the front doors are open or not, but I think so."

"We'll be right there. Can you get out of the building without being seen?"

"I think so. Please hurry. And get a message to Officer Parks about this if you can."

Marge grabbed Trish's arm and pulled. Trish dropped the receiver in the hook, and they ran on their tiptoes back to the saddling paddock. When the gate screeched again, they heard a man yell, "Who's there? Stop or I'll shoot!"

They ran as fast as they could, down the tunnel, out the gate, and into the car. Trish jammed the key in the ignition and, when the engine roared to life, threw the car into reverse and spun in a tight curve. She slammed her foot to the floor and headed for the exit.

Halfway across the parking lot, a red Corvette swerved across in front of her. Trish cranked the wheel to the right only to be confronted by the broad side of a silver BMW. They were trapped. The sight of a gun sticking out of the BMW's window kept her from reversing out of there.

She looked at her mother. Marge's lips moved. Trish knew she was praying. All Trish could say was "Help, God! Help!"

"Get out of the car." The man in the BMW eased his door open, so his voice carried well.

Trish fought the panic rising in her throat. What could they do? She looked to her mother.

"Just do as he says," Marge answered softly. "Somehow God will protect us."

Trish reached for the door handle.

Flashing red and blue lights at every exit announced the arrival of the police. Before the two in the other cars could even start their engines, they were surrounded.

"Get out of your car with your hands on your head." An officer with a bullhorn gave the instructions.

"Thank you, God. Thank you, thank you," Trish and Marge murmured together, the only words they could think of.

"Trish, are you all right?" Officer Parks reached the van.

She nodded and slowly opened the door. When she stepped out, her knees buckled. The man's quick action kept her from hitting the ground.

"Sorry."

"Shock does that to you. What about you, Mrs. Evanston? You okay?"

Marge laughed a shaky laugh. "Think I'll just stay right here if that's okay with you."

"Fine, ma'am. We'll get these two taken care of and then we'll come for your statement." He gave Trish a hand as she climbed back into the minivan. "Take some deep breaths and let yourself relax. You did one fine job, young lady."

By the time they'd given their information to the officers, Trish and Marge wore matching looks of exhaustion.

"I'll bring these statements by tomorrow for you to sign," Officer Parks said. "Trish, do you think you can drive, or would you rather one of us drove you home? We can do that."

"I think I'm okay now. I'm not shaking anymore. I'm mad. Clear through."

"Not a good time to drive either. How about you, ma'am?"

"We'll be fine. I need to stop and call Patrick, our trainer, and let him know we're all right. He'll be sending a rescue squad out any time now."

"If you're sure?"

"See you tomorrow." Trish turned the ignition and pressed the electronic button to roll up the windows. She very carefully put the van in gear and eased out of the parking lot. By the time she reached the on ramp to I-5, she felt almost normal.

Curt was parked in their drive when they arrived. He'd heard about the arrest on the police scanner.

Brad and Patrick met them at the front door, so the five of them gathered around the table where Trish could tell her story. When she finished, Patrick shook his head.

"Lord love ye, lass, what'll it be takin' to keep ye out of trouble?"

Trish looked at her mother, and both of them broke into giggles. One by one the others chimed in.

When they all wiped their eyes, Marge pushed herself to her feet. "I'm calling for pizza—delivered. How hungry are all of you?" She looked from Brad to Curt and shook her head. "Silly question. How about a supreme and a Canadian bacon with pineapple, both large?" At their nods, she went to the phone. She called from the counter by the door. "Trish, you got any coupons?"

Trish sighed. Everything was back to normal. She looked around the room and from face to face of the three men talking, discussing what might happen next at Portland Meadows. Normal sounded heavenly. "I don't think so."

When the doorbell rang a few minutes later, Trish assumed it was the pizza delivery. Instead a television reporter with a cameraman introduced herself. The pizza truck arrived just as the television people left.

"You're going to be famous over this one," Curt warned after gobbling his pizza and calling in his story. "Bet this hits the front page."

He was right. It hit the front page and the Associated Press wire. When Trish arrived home from a school that buzzed with excitement, the reporter who called her "The Comeback Kid" had called. Trish answered his questions and hung up just in time for the two reporters from the local papers who'd showed up that morning after she left for school.

The afternoon paper carried banner headlines.

"Portland Meadows to Open in Two Weeks." Her picture topped another article about the arrest the night before. "Local Girl Solves Track Mystery" read the headline on that one.

"Thank you, God" seemed so inadequate, but that's all Trish could say.

The next two weeks passed in a whirl of activity. Adam Finley hired a van to bring the horses up from California and flew Firefly back to Kentucky. They moved the horses to the track and prepared for opening day. Sarah's Pride and Gatesby were both to run that day, the filly in the Hal Evanston Memorial Handicap like they'd planned. Half the student body from Prairie High promised to be there to cheer them on. Red called, several times, just to make sure Trish was really all right and then to ask how she was holding up as a celebrity.

Trish rose early to exercise the horses at the track before leaving for school; and by Friday, the lack of sleep and strain of all the excitement gave her a colossal headache.

"Just go to bed." Marge turned back the covers. "After this weekend, we'll have Genie ride for us in the morning."

Trish didn't even argue. Her mother was right. No matter how hard it was to admit, she didn't want to live on this schedule for the next six months.

Saturday morning dawned with a heavy cloud cover and a fifty-fifty chance of rain. Trish sniffed the wind as she trotted Sarah's Pride out on the track to loosen her up. "Please, God, here I am asking for something again, but could you possibly let the sun come out for the races this afternoon? A fast, dry track would be such a great way to start the season."

A light mist shrouded a sun circle while she finished her duties and headed for the track kitchen. She could hardly get through the line for her food, so many people stopped to talk with her. Trainers, bug boys, grooms, owners, everyone commenting on the investigation and how grateful they were the track had opened.

The hubbub sounded more like a party than a normal track morning.

Trish sat with Bob Diego and put her plates out on the table so he could put her tray back. "He sure suckered me in," Diego said when he sat back down. "Here I was introducing the crook around and trying to make him feel welcome. I even took him out to see a ranch I know that's for sale." He shook his head. "How could I be so stupid?"

"Well, he scared me out of a year's growth," Trish grinned at her friend. "Let me tell you, a gun looks different when it's pointed at you than it does on TV. I was so glad to see those patrol cars I nearly cried."

"I thought that attorney was part of this, the way he acted at the council meetings."

"Patrick calls him a do-gooder who just believed the wrong man. Strange that a lawyer got sucked in like that. I thought they knew everything."

"They just think so. His ears must be burning; he's been talked about enough." Diego held up his cup for the waitress to refill it. "Sorry you're not riding for me in the handicap, but I guess it is important for you to ride your own horses. I'll let Genie Stokes give you a run for your money."

Trish finished the last bite of her toast. "That's okay.

With your other one, I have six mounts today anyway."
She waved Patrick over to take her chair. "I gotta get going. See you in the paddock."

By the time the call came for the jockeys to parade
to the saddling paddock for the eighth race, Trish had
won two, had a place and a show, and still had the ninth
to go. Wearing the crimson and gold silks of Runnin' On
Farm, Trish fell in behind the others. She weighed in,
thanked the official for his good wishes, and tried to
swallow the butterflies doing their grandstand perform-
ance in her middle.

Why was this race scarier than the others? After all,
she'd walked this path four times already today. She
smiled at the crowd and waved to a group of crimson-
and-gold-garbed students hanging on the rail.

"Tri—cia, Tri—cia, Tri—cia." They turned her name
into a two-syllable chant.

David boosted her aboard and patted her knee. "Give
it all you got, kid. Sure good to see you up on one of
ours."

"Thanks, David, I'm so glad you could make it home
for this."

"You'll be knowin' what to do." Patrick looked up at
her, a sheen of moisture in his eyes. "Do this one for your
dad."

Trish swallowed and tried to smile at her mother, but
she could feel the wobbles at the edge of her mouth.

"God keep you" was all Marge could say.

Sarah's Pride minced out of the tunnel and tossed
her head when the sun hit her. Trish blinked in the
brightness. God had answered another prayer. While
much of the day the sun played hide-and-seek with the
clouds, now it shone on a dry, fast track.

"Your favorite kind, huh, girl?" Trish patted the sorrel neck and smoothed the filly's slightly darker mane to the left side. Off to the east, Mount Hood waited patiently for its yearly snow cover.

The Prairie students continued their chant.

When they cantered back past the grandstands, Trish raised her whip in acknowledgment. She couldn't quit grinning. But she didn't try very hard.

The filly walked into the number-three slot as if she owned it. Trish focused on the spot between the filly's ears and settled into her saddle. The shot! The flag was up and they were off.

Sarah's Pride broke clean and settled into her stride. Trish took her favorite position slightly off the pace and running easily. She didn't want the filly tired before the final stretch.

With a dry track and all fresh horses, the pace was fast, the seconds ticking past. Coming out of the turn, Trish felt someone coming up on the outside. With three in front of her, she made her move. Stride for stride, the outside horse paced her.

They passed the third runner and then the second.

The other riders went to their whips. Neck and neck, three abreast, they thundered for the finish line.

"Now, girl." Trish swung her whip just once. Sarah's Pride leaped forward, nose straight out. One stride, three, and they crossed the line.

Trish grinned at the rider on her right. Genie Stokes grinned back. Neither of them knew who won. Nor did anyone else.

"And that's a photo finish, ladies and gentlemen," the announcer intoned. "We'll have the results for you shortly. Rarely do you see three so close. Numbers three, five, and seven."

Trish cantered on around the track and walked toward the winner's circle. Gold and bronze chrysanthemums bordered the boxed-in area.

David reached her as number three flashed on the scoreboard to win. "You didn't have to cut it quite so close." He grinned up at her.

"Keeps you on your toes that way, Davy Boy." Trish tapped him on the head with her whip. She raised a hand at the chanting that swelled rather than diminished from her friends at Prairie High.

In the winner's circle, the announcer presented her with the ornate silver cup Runnin' On Farm had donated as a permanent trophy for the race.

"It's only fitting, ladies and gentlemen, that the winner today should be Trish Evanston, daughter of the man we honor. While we didn't plan it this way, it couldn't have worked out better."

The three Evanstons accepted the trophy together. Trish took the mike in her hands and stopped to look out at the crowd. "We nearly didn't have racing here anymore, but justice won out. We've been given a second chance, a second wind, and I—we—thank God for the opportunity. May Portland Meadows continue to provide you racing fans with the sport of kings, and we'll give the only King that counts all the glory. Thank you." She handed the mike back.

Arm in arm, Trish, David, and their mother walked out of the winner's circle and into the circle of all their friends and fans. *What a start to a new year,* Trish thought. *Today really is a second wind.*